LACEY AND THE CHRISTMAS CHÂTEAU

JENNIFER POTTER

Lacey and the Christmas Château
© 2022 Jennifer Potter

The right of Jennifer Potter to be identified as author of this Work has been asserted by her in accordance with the Copyright, Designs and Patents Act 1988.
All rights reserved. No part of this publication may be reproduced, stored in retrieval system, copied in any form or by any means, electronic, mechanical, photocopying, recording or otherwise transmitted without written permission from the publisher. You must not circulate this book in any format.

This book is a work of fiction and, except in the case of historical fact, names, characters, places, and incidents are either the product of the author's imagination or are used fictitiously. Any resemblance to actual persons, living or dead, businesses, companies, events, or locales is entirely coincidental.

Paperback ISBN: 979-8-3229-5732-4

ONE

As she walked down bustling Blake Street, taking in the shop windows full of red baubles and reindeer ornaments, Lacey couldn't help but feel that York really was a wonderful place to live. *Especially* at Christmas time. Every December the old city seemed to dazzle, seemed to wrap its occupants and visitors in a magical cocoon of cascading fairy lights and majestic Christmas trees. Everywhere you looked, gorgeous old buildings – from the ancient York Minster to the tiniest, timber-framed tearoom – were draped with silver-tipped garlands and strings of shimmering snowflakes. The place was even filled with the sounds of Christmas cheer, thanks to the carol singers who congregated on street corners to perform rousing renditions of *O Holy Night* and *Ding Dong Merrily on High*, simply to enchant passers-by. Really, it all added up to such a sparkly, carnival-like atmosphere, Lacey imagined even Scrooge himself would've been hard pressed not to crack a smile if he found himself strolling down *Goodramgate* today!

Mind you, talking of Scrooge ... despite the exuberance of her surroundings, Lacey felt just the teeniest hint of desperation zigzag through her. It was an unpleasant sensation, but one – for a very definite reason – that she was being hit with on a pretty-much-daily-basis at the moment. Its presence reminded her that, no matter how much she wanted to, she wouldn't be able to *completely* abandon herself to the festive season this year...

'Hey. Are you OK? You've gone quiet.'

Next to her, her best friend Ella broke off from debating ideas of what she should buy her boyfriend, Olly, for Christmas ("One big present, like the cordless grass trimmer he keeps hinting he wants for the garden? Or lots of little things, so he has loads of gifts to open?"), to shoot her a concerned glance.

'Oh, I'm just taking everything in,' Lacey quickly replied, waving her hand at some pretty star decorations hanging above them. The forlorn feeling she'd just experienced was, after all, not a particularly welcome visitor at any moment, never mind on a jolly day like today. She wasn't about to share it with anybody else and bring down the sparkling mood!

'It's all so gorgeous, isn't it?' Ella agreed. She wrapped her arm through Lacey's. 'I'm so glad we planned to meet up today. I haven't bought a single present yet, so I really need to get organised. Not to mention,' a smile of utter delight filled her face as she glanced down at the pram she was pushing with her free hand, 'that this is Lina's *very first* Christmas shopping trip! How special is that?!'

They both paused on the street to peer at the sleeping baby, nestled in a white fleece blanket in her carrycot.

Meet Lina. Lina, who was Ella's first baby. At nine months old, she was adorable: she had plump cheeks, a little headful of jet black hair, currently hidden under an ivory beanie hat, and stunning grey-blue eyes.

Not that she was always as serene as she was in this moment, Lacey had to admit. In fact, when she was awake she could be really quite the little imp: she thought it funnier to hurl building blocks around Ella's living room than actually stack them in any sort of order; screamed her way through every bath time (even sweet-scented bubbles and the friendliest of rubber ducks couldn't change her mind that Baths Were Evil!); and had already perfected a *so-not-impressed* scowl for when mummy or daddy wanted her to do something she didn't quite fancy (like eat a carrot chunk or two).

Still. None of that stopped Lacey's heart from melting like gooey caramel in a hot pan every time she so much as glanced at the little girl...

'It's *really* special,' she agreed. Then – not able to help herself – she reached out and stroked Lina's teeny-tiny warm tummy. A sigh of longing almost left her lips as she did so, but she managed to hold it back.

They set off along the street again. But it wasn't long before Ella came to another stop. This time it was to gawp at the window of a baby store, the frontage of which was painted in the sweetest butter-yellow.

As her mate drooled over the penguin-print pyjamas and polar bear cuddly toys inside, all artfully set out on a bed of artificial snow, Lacey was hit with a feeling of déjà-vu. She quickly realised why: she and Ella, they'd stood together outside this very baby shop once before, hadn't they? She recognised the place, thanks to its distinctive yellow window frames.

That had been a long time ago, though.

Long before Lina had come on the scene...

'Oh, I *have* to get something for Lina from here! I want a special outfit for Christmas Day, seeing as this will be her *first ever* Christmas with us. And this shop looks like it's got the most gorgeous things to choose from–'

Ella suddenly broke off from the excited spiel she'd launched into. She snapped her head to Lacey, guilt shining in her grey eyes.

'I'm sorry. I shouldn't have ... that is ... would you *mind* if we look inside this place? It's totally fine if you don't want to, though. I can come back another day.'

Lacey swallowed. She knew some people might find it confusing why her mate thought she had to ask permission to browse this particular store. And of course, she didn't. She was simply being thoughtful. Because she and Ella – they'd been friends for so long, ever since primary school – that they were more like sisters than mates. And that meant her friend often knew what was on her mind, without her having to utter a word...

As she'd been musing moments earlier, though, Lacey was determined not to let things that were going on in her life spoil this lovely Christmassy day for anyone else. So, 'Of course it's fine!' she exclaimed.

'Really?'

'Absolutely! Let's go inside.'

Still, her friend hesitated. A silence fell between them, broken only by the chatter and footsteps of the shoppers streaming along the street behind them. And then Ella waved meaningfully at her pram.

'I know I've said this a million times but ... it will happen for you,' she murmured quietly. 'I'm certain about that.'

Lacey couldn't help but give her a woeful smile. 'I don't know if you remember but – I said something very similar to you, once. Outside this very shop, actually.'

Ella looked between her and the baby store's signage with a frown. And then her face cleared.

'Yes! You did. I remember! You said, when the time was right, that I'd have my own little family. And look where we are now!'

They both stared down at Lina again. As she did Lacey remembered how, in the day of her memories, Ella certainly hadn't had the joy on her face she was showcasing now. Instead, she'd been gazing into the baby shop with a pining, sad look in her eyes.

A look *she* was probably mirroring right now, Lacey rued.

There'd been a reason, of course, for Ella's sorrow back then: basically, she'd been broody for the longest time, but had never been lucky with guys. She'd never managed to meet The One, had never tumbled into the kind of madly-in-love relationship that could lead to settling down, to starting a family. In fact, at one point she'd been quite gloomy about her chances of *ever* having the child she so craved.

But then Olly had come along. And look how everything had changed with his arrival on the scene!

Lacey's eyes flickered over the lovely Lina once more, and she felt *soo* glad for her friend, that her life was finally panning out just the way she wanted it to. Really, what could make for a lovelier Christmas than what Ella had now?! An adoring boyfriend; a heart spilling over with all the love that came with being a mother; the sweetest baby to coo and fuss over; all to a backdrop of gifts and good food and a snug, happy home?!

That ... that certainly wasn't the Christmas she and her husband, Daniel, were going to have, Lacey knew. Or, at least, they weren't going to have *all* those things to enjoy, come December 25th...

'You guys – you just need to give it a bit more time, too,' Ella continued earnestly.

Lacey tried not to wince as her own former words were parroted back to her. She knew her mate meant well, the same way she had, when she'd made that remark to Ella a couple of years or so ago. And, of course, time had indeed brought her friend what she'd so desperately wanted: Lina being here, in the flesh, was more than proof of that! So there was sense in what she was saying. Of course there was.

But if *Daniel* was here ... Lacey could already see in her mind's eye how he'd react to that comment of Ella's. How he'd leap nervously from foot to foot and gulp repeatedly, his Adam's apple bobbing furiously up and down in his throat as he tried to hide the panic that was so easily triggered off in him these days...

The image made her heart wobble with a funny mix of both sympathy and guilt.

Oh. Two years into their marriage and this wasn't where she'd expected them to be!

Inside the baby store, where a sprightly version of *Jingle Bells* was playing over the speakers, she and Ella browsed racks of tiny, puffed-skirt dresses and cute cotton cardigans, looking for the perfect Christmas-day outfit for Lina ("It has to be gorgeous, because we'll be taking a million photos of her on the day!"). Lacey couldn't help the pang of envy she felt as her mate picked up adorable outfit after adorable outfit, trying to make her choice.

The thing was – in case it wasn't already obvious from her longing looks at Lina – she and Daniel really wanted to be in the same position as Ella and Olly. They'd desperately hoped, in fact, that they too would be celebrating a first Christmas with their own little one this year. Which sometimes felt strange, because it wasn't so very long ago Lacey had had serious doubts about becoming a mother. Doubts that had stemmed from demons and happenings in her past. Demons she'd had to find a way of facing, for the sake of both herself *and* her marriage.

But face them, she had. And after that, it was like a dam in her heart had burst open. She'd been left hankering for a child of her own with a breathless intensity, the likes of which she'd never experienced before. In fact, sometimes her body would now literally ache with longing to feel a baby growing inside of it!

Daniel, on the other hand, hadn't had any of the doubts she'd carried on her shoulders. Which meant he'd been broody for quite a bit longer than she had, something that showed itself on a daily basis: Lacey often caught him enviously eying packs of nappies in other people's supermarket trolleys; and sometimes had to coax him away from babies they met out-and-about, for fear his over-eagerness to blow raspberries at their giggling faces might come off as creepy rather than cute to their protective parents!

That baby fever, though, meant he'd been elated when she explained she was finally on the same page as him when it came to starting a family. That had been just over a year ago, now; and after that conversation, they'd wasted no time in trying to make their now-joint dream of a child of their own come to fruition.

Oh, those early months of trying to fall pregnant had been such a sweet period in their marriage! Lacey recalled. Life had felt exciting; especially when it came to the actual, getting-down-to-it, business of making a baby! Her cheeks flushed as she remembered the way they'd barely been able to keep their hands off one another through those first few cycles. The long afternoons they'd spent entwined together under the duvet. The way they'd laughed and cuddled as she'd lain, afterwards, with her legs in the air; something she knew wasn't strictly necessary but, at the same time, felt like such a happy and definite sign of claiming the future she'd once thought to be off-limits to her, on account of those demons she'd mentioned earlier.

But then...

Lacey's shoulders slumped. She walked a few feet away from Ella, to where there was a shelving unit, at the back of the store. There, she picked up a copy of a book titled *Getting Ready to Meet Your New Arrival!*, and ran her trembling fingers over the cover.

But then the months had passed, hadn't they? One, after the other, after the other.

And nothing had happened.

Nothing. At. All.

After Ella finally made her choice on Lina's outfit – a sweet red pinafore dress with contrasting cream, cable-knit tights – they left the baby shop and moved into the heart of the city, where York's yearly Christmas market was in full swing. It was a market that spanned much of the length of Parliament Street and was famous for the rows of cute wooden chalets, dressed with garlands and glistening tinsel, many of the traders were housed in. On display were all sorts of enticing products for sale, from personalised tree decorations to handmade bars of soaps scented with warming, winter-y fragrances like spiced orange and cranberry. Other stalls sold street food that would make the perfect pick-me-up for the nip of the December day: hot mulled wine, coffee, fresh crêpes filled with cream and chocolate spread. The air smelt of sweet sugar and cinnamon; and, everywhere you looked, Christmas shoppers in woollen gloves and cheery pom-pom hats were rosy-cheeked and grinning at the thrill of the festive atmosphere.

Despite her wobbly moment at the baby boutique, Lacey's mood was lifted, too, by the bustling, happy atmosphere. She and Ella wandered around, *oohing* over sparkly necklaces on a jewellery stand, and snapping up stocking fillers of chilli jam and bags of fudge for family and friends. Then Lina woke up and they took her to see the Victorian fairground carousel that had been set up for kids (and kids-at-heart!) to ride in the middle of the fair: it was *soo* adorable to see her big eyes widen in amazement as she watched the painted horses dance and spin on their golden poles.

After that, they were just about to retreat to the warmth of a café – Lina was ready for a lunchtime feed – when Lacey spotted somebody she knew, hovering in front of a liquor stall in distinctive purple welly boots and a leopard-print puffa jacket. Actually, not just hovering: the woman seemed to be rather determinedly twisting the arm of the frazzled-looking stall owner, judging by the part of their conversation that drifted over to Lacey:

'I know I've tried four types already, but the passion fruit flavour sounds *to die for*. Come on, dear, it is Christmas – surely you can let a little old lady have one more free sample?'

Lacey smiled wryly to herself as she approached the stand, just in time to see the woman – who happened to be her grandma, Rose – knocking back a taster pot of something that *definitely* looked alcoholic in nature...

'Grandma? Hi! I didn't know you'd be here today! What are you up to? A bit of Christmas shopping?' Lacey looked quizzically between Rose and the liquor stall and saw, with one glance at the signage, that it housed a flavoured-gin trader.

'Lacey!' A beam appeared on Rose's face. She pulled her granddaughter into a big hug, before muttering in her ear: 'I've never known a market give away so much free alcohol – I've already had three free shots out of the vodka stand. One of them was even candy-cane flavoured! What better way to get in the festive mood?!'

Lacey couldn't help but laugh. 'You'll be getting tipsy! I'll have to see you safely home at this rate.'

Rose waved a hand dismissively. 'Ah, at my age I'd have to knock back quite a few more rounds of gin before I got even nicely squiffy!' Her eyes snapped back to the bottles lining the stand. 'So maybe I could wangle *another* taster, that passion fruit flavour really was divine– Oh.' She blinked, noticing the stall owner had suddenly disappeared from view. 'Where's the man gone? He must have wandered off.'

He hadn't, actually. Lacey had spotted him just moments earlier, nervously ducking down out of sight behind the counter. She smiled to herself. Clearly he felt a little defenceless against Rose and her "little-old-lady" routine, and wanted to protect what was left of his gin supply for other potential customers!

'Best press on, then. Plenty more stands to visit,' Rose nodded. 'Oh, you're with Ella! Ella! Hello, dear. How's the little one doing?'

Rose walked over to greet Ella and Lina. Before she did, though, she bent down and picked up something that had been lying by her feet. Something which left Lacey blinking in surprise. Because ... well, because it was a rather enormous *black bin liner* that her grandma had suddenly lifted and lugged over her shoulder. Which, given the sparkle and glitter they were surrounded by, looked really awfully strange. Not the most Christmassy of items by any stretch of the imagination!

'Er, grandma?' Lacey scratched her head then pointed at Rose's strange baggage. 'What's that you're carrying around? It looks heavy. Can I help you with it?'

'Tsk, no, I'm absolutely fine, dear. And never you mind what's in here.' Rose shook the bag then winked at Ella, who laughed. 'Let's just say – it's a surprise.'

'Oh. OK,' Lacey shrugged bemusedly. She knew better than to press further; her grandma lived life in her own very particular way, after all. Which was a trait Lacey admired, even if it meant she didn't always understand what surprising scheme Rose might have lurking up her sleeve next. (Last year, it'd been to head off on a wild coach trip through Europe, one which had involved zip wiring, sea kayaking and the drinking of multiple kinds of cocktails en route – all despite her being well into her seventies!)

'Well, we're heading off to find a nice café. Do you want to join us for a cuppa?'

'A cuppa?!' Rose looked at her as aghast as though she'd suggested they all go and ride the carousel stark-naked. 'When I've just been supping fine gin? No thanks, dear. It'll spoil the after-taste. Besides,' she winked again, and nodded at her mysterious bin liner, 'I'm too busy to stop. Put it this way, I've *lots* to accomplish today... Although I might make one tiny last detour to that drink stand over there – because they're putting Baileys in their hot chocolate! Oh, before I go though, will I see you at F-Group this week?'

Now, the mention of F-Group – which was a local women's rights organisation her mum, Sadie, and her grandma supported – might not seem an especially Christmassy topic for Rose to have dropped into their conversation. In fact, the subject of F-Group in general was something Lacey used to avoid as best she could, given she'd once found the idea of a feminist club a little intimidating (made more so by the active campaigns its rather determined members like to immerse themselves in: for example, last year they'd all travelled to London to join in a noisy, national "*Unfinished Business*" rally to highlight ongoing unfair issues in the UK, like the startling fact women *still* didn't earn equal pay to men!). It was only after she'd unwittingly become involved in one of their crusades – to try and have a local lap dancing club closed down – that she'd come to appreciate the group's passion, to respect the values they were fighting for. Not that she could count herself as a regular member of its ranks, though: generally she was too busy with work and life in general to go to their weekly meetings. This winter, however, she'd found out via her mum that the group had something very special – and very festive indeed – up their sleeve.

Something so special, she'd decided to *make time*, so she could once again play a part in their latest exploits...

'Yes, I'll be there, grandma.'

'Good girl,' Rose nodded. She threw out a salute then headed off ... but not before nearly knocking a bewildered fellow shopper to the ground, thanks to an over-exuberant swing of her bulky black bin liner as she marched off.

Lacey ran over to check the lady was OK (she was, despite the expressive *oof* sound she'd made when Rose's bag had smacked her squarely in the face!). Then she and Ella shared a wry smile as they watched her grandma heading determinedly towards the hot-choc-with-Baileys stall...

Next up on Lacey and Ella's schedule was the café stop they'd just mentioned to Rose. Before they left the market, though, Lacey discreetly purchased a bottle of the passion-fruit-flavoured gin her grandma had been lusting over. It would make a perfect Christmas gift for Rose, along with perhaps a chunky knit scarf or some new winter gloves, Lacey decided. Then she and her mate headed through the streets to the place that was their favourite hangout in York these days: a hip coffee shop called The Bluebird.

Inside, retro *Merry Christmas* signs on brass chains had been hung along the café's exposed brickwork, and the sleek serving counter was dotted with flickering lanterns. It all made for a chic but snug atmosphere – especially given that the cast iron radiators were turned on full blast, providing much-welcome heat to all the customers scurrying in from the bitter December weather outside!

They settled into some comfy black armchairs near the window. Lacey was glad to unravel her tasselled scarf from her neck, and wriggle out of her thick parka. As she did so, though, she noticed Ella look over at her and frown, in a concerned-kind-of-a-way. Which was a bit strange – Lacey quickly glanced down, wondering if she had a stain on her jumper or something like that. Everything looked OK, though, so she was about to ask Ella what was wrong, when she got distracted by a server bringing over some menus.

'Well. I already know what I want – all your grandma's talk of hot chocolate means that's exactly what I feel like! Although I'll have mine with marshmallows rather than Baileys,' Ella laughed, as she unstrapped Lina from her pram and sat her on her lap. 'And I'm *definitely* having a toasted teacake with loads of strawberry jam, too.' She mock-shivered. 'I need warming up after walking round the market in the freezing cold. How about you?'

Hot chocolate? Marshmallows? Strawberry jam? Oh. Lacey's mouth watered at the mention of all those sweet treats. But she quickly shook her head and searched the menu for the herbal tea section instead.

'Oh, I just fancy a ... a ginger tea, actually,' she lied. 'Ginger is warming, isn't it?' she added, with a bright smile.

Ella hesitated. Even Lina paused in her adorable babbling and stared at her, as though astounded anyone could pass on options as yummy as a hot chocolate or a toasted teacake!

'Well, yes. I suppose it is. But,' her mate looked at her uncertainly, 'is that *all* you're having? Don't you fancy a piece of cake or something, too?' She pointed to the serving counter, where all sorts of delicious concoctions were laid out for customers to choose from, from gooey brownies to big fat chunks of walnut cake.

Lacey quickly averted her eyes from the temptations on display. 'I'm fine. The tea will do me nicely.'

'But' Ella scratched her head and looked a bit uncomfortable, 'Lacey, honestly. You ... you look like you could do with eating a *whole cake*, never mind just one slice.'

Lacey's eyebrows shot up. Er, what now? That was an awfully strange thing to say, wasn't it? Before she could ask her mate what she meant by that comment, though, Ella spoke up again.

'Why don't you let me treat you?' her mate offered, her face earnest. 'Pick anything you want. Anything at all.'

'Aw thank you. That's such a kind offer. But – honestly! All I want is a cup of tea!' Lacey insisted.

And then, when their order arrived, she did everything she could not to look at Ella's side of the table. She tried not to slide an envious glance at the towering hot chocolate the server set in front of her mate. Tried not to think of how cute and delicious it looked, especially given the mini gingerbread man they'd topped the whipped cream with. She tried, too, not to inhale the mouth-watering smell of the hot butter melting over Ella's toasted teacake.

In years gone past, sharing a few indulgent treats with her mate had always made the perfect end to a Christmas shopping spree.

But not today. Not this year.

Because this year, things were different. She'd already reflected on that fact, hadn't she? Had already considered earlier, that she wouldn't be able to throw herself into December festivities the way she used to. Because if she *did*...

A picture of her husband's gorgeous face popped into her mind. It was a face she loved dearly. Only, these days, it seemed to be permanently etched with angst.

She was determined to do everything she could not to add to that angst. Forgoing a hot chocolate, a slice of cake ... those things were a small – no make that a *tiny* price to pay, she nodded guiltily – for the sake of her husband's peace of mind.

For the sake of giving them *both* the best chance of snaring the future they wanted; prayed for; should perhaps even write a pleading note to Santa Claus himself, for...

TWO

A few miles away, while Lacey and Ella were hanging out in The Bluebird café, Daniel was on the outskirts of the city, busy at work. He didn't have to work *every* Saturday of the month; but being supervisor of a gift shop at a grand old stately home (which used to be a private residence, but was now open for visitors to explore), meant he had to cover at least some of them. He didn't mind, though. He thought of his wife, who was currently browsing festive offerings with her friend in the centre of York: he would have Monday off in return for working today and – seeing as Lacey would be back at work then – was planning to use the time to do a little Christmas shopping of his own!

He turned from the shop counter to look out of the tall sash window behind him. Grace Hall was a Georgian manor house with suitably decadent grounds to match, meaning he always had a lovely view from the gift shop, situated as it was in a lofty room at the back of the hall. It was a landscape, seeing as he'd worked here for a year-and-a-half or so now, that Daniel had come to know well. In that time he'd watched the gorgeous gardens outside weave their way through the different seasons: he loved the way they bloomed in spring, with bright bluebells and cheery tulips, but wasn't *quite* so keen on the barrenness winter cast over the place. There were still pretty evergreens and bushes full of bright red berries, of course. But there were also lots of shrivelled shrubs and naked trees with bare branches, branches the cool wind was whistling through today.

Despite the fact it was cosy in the gift store, he shivered at the sight. And then he felt a beat of worry as he thought of Lacey. He hoped she wasn't getting too cold as she walked around the city today. She needed to look after herself, he nodded. In fact – he suddenly got an idea for some stocking fillers for his wife. He could buy her some of those thick woollen socks hikers liked to wear, couldn't he? And maybe some new gloves, too, the big fat insulated ones you found in camping shops. Just to make sure she kept toasty this winter, because the last thing he wanted – or that they *needed*, he fretted – was for her to fall sick with the flu or a cold or a ... a chill. Not, he considered, scratching his head, that he was really sure if catching "a chill" was still a thing, these days? It sounded more like an ailment that would befall an old Victorian dear, who only had a moth-eaten blanket and a solitary candle stump to keep her warm through the English winter nights.

Anyway. He got distracted, then, by a customer – a plump lady with a bobbed haircut, chunky gold earrings, and a big beaming smile – bringing an armful of merchandise to the counter. He quickly rang her items through the till. This looked a good sale! he mused, watching the *Total Due* figure tally up.

Not that that was an unusual thing in this store, he had to admit. Their visitors often left with plenty of souvenirs of their trip!

'Find everything you were looking for?' he checked.

'I certainly did!' the lady nodded. Her eyes shone as he popped all her purchases into a Grace Hall paper bag. 'We only came here for a day out – I've been wanting to have a nosey around this lovely old place for ages, haven't I, John?' She nodded at the man standing next to her, who smiled indulgently. 'But thanks to your beautiful gift shop, I've also got a huge chunk of my Christmas shopping done in one fell swoop. I know it's only early in December, but it's nice to be organised, isn't it? So whoever your buyer is, please thank them from me. They have *fabulous* taste!'

Oh. Well. That would be *him*, Daniel thought, with a flash of pride.

'We're off to your tearoom next,' the man added, looking happy at the thought. 'I hope they do a fine lunch.'

'They definitely do,' Daniel told him. 'In fact – the food is awesome!'

They both looked delighted at that, and headed off in a flurry of smiles and calls of "Happy Holidays!"

As he watched them go, Daniel felt a flush of pleasure – not something he often felt these days, he realised. But who wouldn't be at least *a little* happy at being told they had *fabulous taste*?! He walked out from behind the counter and, with his hands on his hips, looked around the shop. It did look pretty great in here, he nodded – if he was allowed to say so himself, seeing as he was pretty much 100% responsible for the store's image and contents!

Over the past couple of months, the stock of the summer – floral-print gardening gloves and bottles of organic cordials – had given way to new products, that he'd sourced from trade fairs and online catalogues. Now, the shelves were packed with all things Christmas-related: snow globes and stockings, figurines of angels and elves. There was even a display of scented candles, boasting all manner of festive fragrances, that made the shop smell enticingly of spiced apples and peppermint creams. He'd hung strings of white shimmering stars from the sash windows, and put up a tree in the centre of the room, draped with metallic beads and silver lights, to pull everything together. The rest of the store had been taken over with items he thought would make perfect gifts for the season: gemstone earrings, fancy hand creams, *Built A Mini Snowman!* kits for kids.

Yes. It all looked so cheery, he wasn't surprised it'd gotten that lady and her partner in the mood for some Christmas shopping! To think, too, he hadn't been sure he was the right man for the job, when the post of *Gift Shop Supervisor* at Grace Hall had been offered to him by the lovely Lady Tuncaster herself – mainly because, although he had a background in retail, he used to specialise in selling sportswear, not the chintzy china and cherry churd he assumed visitors to a stately home would want to buy! When his life had been hit by a curveball last year, though – in the form of the sports shop he used to own, Track & Trainers, going under – he hadn't been left with much choice but to grab whatever job came his way.

Thankfully, it hadn't taken him long to realise he actually felt very at home at Grace Hall. Not that his time working here had been completely stress-free, he had to admit. Not if you included the, er–

Well, the ... the *unsettling incidents*, he supposed you'd call them, that'd happened to him since being connected with the old house.

Out of the blue, sounds and images flashed through his mind: moss-covered gravestones from long ago; the haunting melody of an old French nursery rhyme; violet ribbons woven through dark ringlets...

He swallowed then glanced warily around the quiet store, a little freaked out, suddenly. But his gaze continued to be met with a room full of Christmas cheer and nothing more.

Thank goodness, he nodded quickly.

Thank goodness indeed...

Realising that he was letting his thoughts go to a place they probably shouldn't, Daniel gave himself a shake, then determinedly returned to reminiscing about his job. About the way he'd quickly learnt what his new customers wanted to buy. The way he'd come to realise he had a bit of a talent for setting out quirky displays of notecards and noodle bowls. Of how quickly he'd come to love his new role. Of how he felt very privileged, to be greeted each morning – as he headed down the estate's snaking driveway – by a striking view of Grace Hall's stone pillars and elegant turrets, rising into the sky. It certainly beat turning up to work at some soulless factory!

And yet...

And yet, despite all those positives *and* the praise his last customer had just thrown his way, Daniel could feel something heavy returning to his shoulders. It wasn't anything to do with recalling the "unsettling incidents" that'd happened in his life since being linked to the hall, though. No, this was something else. Something, he sighed, that seemed to be his companion 24/7 at the moment. A huge, stubborn, hanging-over-his-head cloud that, if he dared examine too closely, made him feel as jittery and on edge as though he'd just downed a triple shot espresso...

Even simply acknowledging that cloud's existence caused him to chew nervously at the inside of his cheek. And then his eyes stole in a direction he didn't really *want* to look in: namely, at the *Gifts for Children* display – a shelving unit crammed with cuddly toys, colouring books and candy necklaces – to the left of him.

Daniel hesitated. Then, even though he knew it was a bad idea, he found himself wandering across the wooden floor towards those very shelves. His attention snapped straight to a new product that'd arrived last week: a box of *the cutest* Christmas-pudding-print bibs you've ever set eyes on.

He glanced over his shoulder, making sure he was still alone. And then – even though, once again, he knew he shouldn't, that it wasn't a wise thing to do – he picked up one of the bibs and held the tiny scrap of fabric in his hand. As he stared down at it, he felt a gnawing pain in his heart.

Oh.

Oh.

He imagined a teeny tot wearing the item on Christmas Day. Sitting on a highchair, adorable face smeared with mashed potato as its doting parents giggled and cooed and looked lovingly at one another, sharing their delight at the little miracle they were raising. It was such a sweet image, he even felt his eyes begin to well up…

'Daniel, love! How's your morning been?'

Just at that, someone burst through the shop door, making him jump – namely, Joanne, from the administrative team. She – along with a girl called Lily from accounts – covered the shop during his lunch breaks and days off.

She came over to stand next to him. 'Time for your lunch, so off you pop. Ooh, what's that you've got?'

Daniel blushed as she tugged the bib out of his hand.

'How cute! I might have to nab one of these for my granddaughter. Speaking of which–' she looked around, her face thoughtful '–while you're gone I'm going to see what other Christmas presents I can buy from here. May as well make use of our staff discount, right?!' She winked then frowned. 'Oh dear, are you feeling OK? You look awfully flushed, love.'

That remark made Daniel's face grow even hotter. He was glad, though, that Joanne didn't seem to have cottoned on he was *flustered*, rather than flushed. Had been, in fact, from the moment she'd walked in on him; which didn't really make any sense because it wasn't like she'd caught him throwing out a few moves to Mariah Carey's "All I Want for Christmas Is You" in the middle of the shop or anything like that! All he'd been doing was gawping at a perfectly innocent baby bib. Although, he supposed, when you put it like that … perhaps that *did* sound a bit of a weird thing to have been doing. Hm.

Really, he should've been sensible and stayed away from the kids' display stand altogether! he chided himself. Then, after dabbing discreetly at his damp eyes with his sleeve, he told Joanne he was fine. Absolutely fine!

She hesitated. Looked between him and the bib, now clasped in her hand. And then she reached out and patted his arm.

'Go and have your lunch, love. And … take as much time as you need, OK?' she added gently. 'I'm in no rush to get back to the office.'

By the time he made it to the staff kitchen, Daniel's hot blush had retreated – helped along, no doubt, by the fact he had to walk outside and get chilled-to-the-bone by the icy winds, just to reach his destination. The kitchen and staff break room, you see, were housed not in the hall itself, but in a separate barn conversion – a double-height, red-brick building, set just across the gravel drive – which also contained staff offices *and* Grace Hall's on-site café, aptly named The Old Barn Tearoom.

He was just grabbing a fork from the cutlery drawer and getting ready to settle down at the table with his lunch box, when somebody else walked into the kitchen.

'Afternoon, Daniel. And what a jolly afternoon it is. Just the kind we like to have here at Grace Hall! Lots of visitors, and nearly every single one bought a guide book today! It's really quite wonderful. I hope they've all been spending as generously in the gift shop, too?'

Daniel turned, to see he'd been joined by Neville, the House Steward and his boss, into the bargain. Neville's job was basically to be the "man-in-charge" at the hall. He oversaw everything that went on and, with his solid knowledge of all-things-historical, also ran a lot of the guided tours. He was an older man, but still had a headful of mousy brown hair; and he always looked smart, in a conservative, neat shirt and tie. Except ... the tie his boss was wearing today actually *wasn't* very conservative at all, Daniel suddenly noticed. The reason being, it had colourful, cartoon penguins printed all over it – clearly a nod to the festive month they'd just slipped into.

Hm. As Daniel eyed the unexpected addition to the House Steward's wardrobe, he realised the cheery tie actually suited Neville. Admittedly, on most blokes it would probably look cheesy, but – probably on account of his endearingly-jovial personality – Neville seemed able to carry it off!

Not that he could recall his boss wearing anything so overtly-Christmassy last December, he considered. He wondered if the tie was an outward sign of the happy-change-in-life-circumstances he knew Neville had gone through since then. A change, he nodded, that was *very good* for his boss ... but perhaps not *quite* so good for him, Daniel acknowledged ruefully. In fact, he had to bite back a sigh as he thought of how, although he mostly got on well with his boss, those changes in Neville's life meant the pair of them ended up bumping into each other outside of work these days – on a *way more regular basis* than Daniel was sure he was really comfortable with...

His forehead creased in a frown at the thought, but he quickly tried to push his misgivings aside. Because, really – Lacey flashed into his mind – he had enough to focus on right now, without adding Neville, and his, er, unexpected intrusion into his private life these days, into the mix.

'Yes. It's been a good day so far,' he nodded, in reply to his boss's question about the gift shop. He thought of the generous haul his last customer had walked out of the store with. People *did* seem to be in a spending mood at the moment. Probably something to do with the Christmas season.

Neville beamed at him. 'Excellent news! Now, can I make you a cup of tea?' He switched on the kettle. 'I'm having a quick break before the next guided tour. And,' he retrieved something from the fridge, 'I've a box of these yummy little chaps for us to enjoy, too! Would you like one– oh.'

It was Neville's turn to blush, as he thrust – then quickly removed – a box of treats from right under Daniel's nose. But not before Daniel had time to recognise what his boss had been offering him: the container held a batch of mini jam-and-cream sponge cakes. Delicious delicacies indeed, he thought wistfully. And ones he was awfully familiar with – given he knew they'd been baked by his very own mum, Hazel...

'Sorry, sorry. I forgot you're not eating things like this at the moment,' Neville winced. He peered over his glasses at the open Tupperware container in Daniel's hand. 'I'm sure you have something much more appetising for lunch anyway! Looks like, er–' He scratched his head, clearly trying to work out *what*, exactly, Daniel was about to get stuck into.

'It's a bulgur wheat salad,' Daniel explained. 'With pumpkin seeds. And black beans. And, yes, it's,' he nodded, as adamantly as he could, '*super yummy*!' To demonstrate that point, he shoved a forkful into his mouth and forced a grin to his face as he swallowed down the oil-free, parsley-laden concoction.

'I ... I'm sure it is!' Neville agreed. There was only the slightest hint of dubiousness on his face as he added: 'Why would you even want one of these cakes when you can have bulg– er, what was it again?'

'Bulgur wheat.'

'Bulgur wheat! Exactly. Wonderful stuff, that sounds!' he rallied generously. 'Well – enjoy!'

As Neville took his cup of tea and cakes and headed off to his office, Daniel put down his fork and picked bits of parsley out of his teeth. As he did, visions of his boss's box of jam sponges danced in front of his eyes, and he couldn't help but sigh. Couldn't help but think, too, of the tearoom next door, where his last customers had been headed. He wondered what *they* were scoffing back right now – not a cold salad, that was for sure, he mused, with a rueful glance at his Tupperware box. No. Given he knew the café had an array of wintery treats on the menu this month, they'd be far more likely to be enjoying hot roast potatoes and gravy, or creamy garlic mushrooms on toast, or even an indulgent sticky toffee pudding with custard.

Oh, man.

For a moment, Daniel very nearly started drooling. But then he squared his shoulders and picked up his fork again.

Those thoughts – they were a sign of weakness. And weakness would get him – *and* Lacey – nowhere. He had to be strong. Have a bit of willpower. One day things would be different. They definitely would be, he tried to reassure himself – even as his heart wobbled with doubt.

But until then, bulgur wheat 'n pumpkin seed salads – with all the zinc and fibre and manganese and vitamin A they boasted – were going to play a *way* more important part in his life than the melt-in-your-mouth whipped cream filling of his mum's mini sponge cakes.

A *way more important* part indeed, he nodded determinedly.

THREE

When his lunch break was finished, Daniel headed back across the gravelled drive and made his way into the rear entrance of the hall. But just as he was about to return to the gift store, something caught his attention.

A faint sound, of laughter – a woman's delighted laughter, that was – drifted down the corridor towards him. Which might not seem a particularly unusual occurrence, but in truth people giggling or chortling wasn't something he heard very often while he was at work. Visitors often seemed awed by the rather grand surroundings a trip to Grace Hall immersed them in, you see; and so tended to murmur to one another in hushed, respectful tones as they moved through their tour of the old house, rather than let out peals of laughter the likes of which he was hearing now.

Daniel looked between the shop and the long, high-ceilinged corridor that joined this part of the hall to the main front rooms. Then, remembering Joanne had said he could take his time over his lunch break, he decided to give in to his intrigue. It would only take a moment, after all, to sneak through the house and find out what was going on, that sounded so amusing!

He walked stealthily along the creaky, original oak floor, passing umpteen panelled doorways and console tables decorated with antique chinoiserie vases, until he reached the room the giggles had been emanating from: Grace Hall's entrance foyer. As he pushed open the double doors leading to that area, though, the laughter abruptly stopped.

He stepped inside and glanced around. Set off to one side of the entrance was a large, solid visitor desk, where tourists bought their tickets and guide books. For some reason it appeared to be currently unmanned – an unusual occurrence, Daniel realised, with a frown. Maybe whoever was working the desk this afternoon had had to pop out for a minute or two? Aside from that, though, the rest of the room looked the same as usual, for this time of year at least. The lights of the huge Christmas tree that had been set up in the middle of the black-and-white marble floor were twinkling merrily; and the gold chandelier hanging from the ceiling looked lavish as always. As for the source of the laughter, though ... as Daniel surveyed the room, he was surprised to find he seemed to be alone. The mystery giggling-woman he'd heard was nowhere to be seen.

Hm. Strange. Oh, well. He shrugged, and was about to turn around and retrace his steps to the shop, when something made him pause.

Hang on...

Set against the left-hand wall of the room was a huge, old stone fireplace, flanked on either side by two lofty columns. And there, out of the corner of his eye, Daniel suddenly saw a flash of movement. He turned his head fully ... only to realise he'd been mistaken to think he was the sole occupant of the entrance hall. Because now he looked more closely he could see that, beside one of the columns – in fact, being partially obscured by one of them, which was why he'd missed him on first glance – a person was hovering.

A man. A stout man wearing–

Er, actually, what *was* he wearing? Daniel frowned. He narrowed his eyes, trying to make sense of the strange and awfully-old-fashioned outfit the bloke was clad in. It comprised: a long white robe, tied at the waist with gold rope. A floor-length, red velvet cloak. A ... a *very* odd looking hat: pointy-shaped, red, decorated with a golden cross. He was also carrying a large golden stick with a scroll-top, of the sort bishops carried around; and, to top off the overall odd appearance, was rocking curly white hair and an enormous white beard. Really, the whole effect was as though some man-of-the-cloth – one from a time long, *long* ago, that was – had suddenly decided to pop up in the 21st century.

Daniel found himself gawping across the room, not quite sure how to interpret what he was seeing. Most male tourists to the hall tended to be dressed in a rather more conventional manner, after all: chinos, shirts, sensible jackets. Not the ... the flowing robes some religious cleric of the past might have sported as he hung out in his cathedral or abbey or wherever it was religious-clerics-of-the-past used to frequent. Really, he thought bemusedly, the sight was so odd, if there'd been mushrooms in his bulgur wheat salad, he'd have been wondering if they'd been of the "magic" variety – because he almost felt like he was tripping out right now!

A beat later, though, and any amusement Daniel was feeling abruptly evaporated. Instead, apprehension stole over him. Because this, he reminded himself, wasn't *the first time* he'd found himself in a situation where he'd thought he might be hallucinating, was it..?

He mind wandered, once more, to thoughts of the "unsettling incidents" he'd experienced since being connected with Grace Hall.

He recalled how *those* incidents had also involved strangers.

Strangers wearing clothing that had hailed from a time long ago...

His heart began to thud, then, harder than it'd done in quite a while. Even more so when he noticed this particular stranger had turned his head, and was now looking *at him*.

Right. At. Him.

As they held each other's gaze, Daniel swallowed. But then the fellow smiled and lifted his hand in greeting. After that, and still clutching his huge golden staff, he began crossing the floor in Daniel's direction, his black boots beating against the marble tiles.

Despite the fact it was the depths of winter, sweat trickled down Daniel's back. With each step the man took towards him, his keenness to turn and run, back to the safety of the gift shop, grew stronger. If only, he rued, he hadn't been so nosy and decided to go snooping around to find the source of the laughter his attention had been caught by. If he hadn't done that, he could be rearranging jars of organic hand cream right now, perfectly oblivious to this creepy, robed-figure wandering around the entrance hall!

But it was too late to go anywhere, because suddenly the bloke was standing right in front of him. So close, Daniel could see the broken veins on his thickset nose, the unkemptness of his shaggy eyebrows, the almost-unnatural fullness of his white curls.

Panic seeped through him. Panic that upped a few more notches as he noticed the man was opening his mouth, in readiness to utter something.

What was he going to say? Who was he going to introduce himself as? And – more importantly – what was he going to want *of him*? Daniel fretted, his hands clenching into anxious fists.

'*Alreet*, lad. How's it going? I'm Stevie.'

Er, what now? As the stranger's words dropped on him, Daniel blinked in surprise. Because he wasn't quite sure what he'd been expecting to hear – but definitely not a hearty Geordie accent. Plus – Stevie? That didn't sound like a particularly medieval name now, did it?!

'Daniel! *Coucou!*'

Oh! Daniel jumped. Because, just then, from across the room, someone unexpectedly called *his* name. Their voice echoed around the high-ceilinged space. At the same time he saw a head pop up from behind the visitor desk, the one he'd thought was unmanned. It was all enough to set a fresh burst of fear-related adrenaline whizzing through his veins. Honestly. He clutched a hand to his chest. What was going *on* this afternoon?!

The person who emerged from behind the depths of the vast desk – who happened to be Lady Tuncaster, the owner of Grace Hall – strode across the floor to join them. Daniel noticed she was wearing black riding boots; cream jodhpurs that were splattered with mud; and that her cheeks were as pink as though she'd been galloping wildly through the neighbouring wheat fields (which, knowing his employer's love for the horses she kept in the estate's stable block, was actually quite a likely scenario). He also noticed, as she crossed the marble tiles, that she was waving her phone in the air.

'Goodness, I feel like I've been squatting behind that desk for ages trying to find this. I was right, though – I *had* left it in one of the drawers! Neville will be cross with me now. I was only supposed to be watching the desk for five minutes ... but instead I've gone and muddled up all his paperwork. Oops!' she tittered.

'Oh, well. Let's get on with taking a photo for our Instagram page,' she continued, looking right at Stevie. 'Actually, before we do– Daniel? Are you quite alright? You look as pale as though you've seen a ghost!' Lady Tuncaster laughed at that last remark, really quite animatedly, even though Daniel didn't find what she'd said amusing at all.

Not, he shuffled in embarrassment, when for a panicked moment there he'd believed that *was* what he was seeing, right here in the entrance hall! Of course, he wouldn't – couldn't – admit that to his employer. It sounded too crazy. It *was* crazy! And yet, it was also a cold hard truth that he had form when it came to seeing people that *weren't of this time*, didn't he?

Thankfully, he nodded, judging from Lady Tuncaster's intention to take a photo of this stranger for the Grace Hall Instagram page, he'd clearly read the situation really quite wrong on this occasion. Indeed, his cheeks went from white to bright red as he realised the bloke he'd thought might be an apparition-from-the-Dark-Ages was actually made up of nothing more sinister than flesh and blood and bushy eyebrows.

Oops.

Still. His embarrassment was swiftly softened by a sense of relief, because the last thing he'd wanted was for this slightly-odd encounter to be yet another of the Grace-Hall-related, unsettling happenings he'd been reflecting on earlier. Thoughts whipped through him: of Lacey; the Christmas baby bib in the shop; even of his flipping bulgur wheat salad. Yup. Right now, he had more than enough going on in his life. He didn't need to add any more difficulties into the mix – especially ones of the spooky variety!

Meanwhile, 'He looks wonderful, doesn't he?' Lady Tuncaster was continuing. 'I'm really quite tickled by how well the costume has turned out.' She let out another peal of laughter as she pointed at Stevie. It was only then that Daniel realised it must have been *her* delighted giggles he'd heard drifting towards the gift shop.

He hesitated, not quite sure why she was *so* taken by this man and his strange outfit.

His employer must have picked up on his perplexed vibe, because she clucked at him. 'Daniel! You don't seem to be in a very festive mood. How can you not agree Stevie here looks simply fabulous as St Nicholas? I think he's going to bring some wonderful Christmas cheer to our visitors this month.'

Oh. St Nicholas??

'He's the original Santa Claus,' Lady Tuncaster explained. 'The 4th century Bishop of Myra, famous for his charity and generosity. So when I saw this outfit online I just *had* to snap it up. I thought to myself: what a novel idea, to have St Nic himself greet our sightseers this December! A lot of them are history buffs, so I thought they'd appreciate the gesture. What do you think, Daniel? Oh, just one moment–' She nodded meaningfully at Stevie, who jumped into action.

'Oh, ay, right.' Stevie cleared his throat and wished Daniel, 'Peace and joy for the holiday season, from all of us at Grace Hall. We hope you have a Christmas filled with blessings!' – lines that were clearly pre-rehearsed, given the way Lady

Tuncaster silently mouthed them at the same time. Then he reached into the pocket of his velvet cloak and retrieved a pretty, ribbon-wrapped bag of chocolate Brazil nuts, which he pressed into Daniel's hand.

'A complimentary gift for our guests,' Lady Tuncaster explained, before breaking into a round of applause. 'That was wonderful, Stevie. He's from a local amateur dramatic club,' she added, to Daniel. 'Plays the role perfectly, don't you think?'

Er. Daniel scratched his head, pretty sure the 4th century Bishop of Myra – wherever that might be – probably *hadn't* rocked a thick Geordie accent. That aside, however, he seemed a cheery fellow and Daniel was sure their guests would appreciate the novelty of bumping into the original Santa Claus himself as they toured Grace Hall this month. Really, he had to say, Lady Tuncaster was a fab hostess. She might only have opened this place to the public to help raise funds to maintain the old building; but no-one could've been more welcoming or keener to make sure visitors enjoyed their time in her home, than his generous-spirited employer.

As for him, though ... as he walked away clutching his bag of chocolate nuts – nuts he wouldn't even be able to eat, thanks to their sugary coating – he realised he didn't feel joy *or* peace. And as for blessings?

Hm. He felt pretty short on those this festive season, too, he admitted, as he tripped back to the gift store. In fact, he came over really quite gloomy indeed as he realised the blessing he'd *hoped* (and prayed and sent umpteen positive messages out into the universe to try and manifest!) just wasn't going to end up in his and Lacey's arms this Christmas.

Another image of the Christmas-pudding-print bib he'd had clasped in his hand before lunch flashed in his mind's eye, causing a muscle to twitch erratically in his cheek. But then he rallied. He reminded himself that, two years ago, he and Lacey had got married (a thought that also reminded him it was their anniversary in a couple of weeks' time, and he hadn't even considered what they might do to celebrate that). At one time, though, he'd thought the gorgeous, winter wedding they'd experienced might never happen, given the difficult spell they'd gone through in their relationship that same year. But against the odds they'd pulled through and made it down the aisle.

Which just showed that lovely things *could* happen ... even when everything seemed stacked against you, he nodded firmly.

That thought, of their second wedding anniversary being just around the corner, made Daniel hesitate once more on his return to the Grace Hall gift shop. This time, though, it was as he walked through the inner hall – which housed an opulent oak staircase – where he came to a stop.

He glanced around. Nearby, there were a couple of older female visitors heading in to view the adjacent Georgian Dining Room. But no staff members who might wonder why he was making yet another detour before he returned to work, this time to the first floor of the hall. The reason being, he'd been hit with a sudden urge to look at something located at the top of the staircase...

He darted up the steps until he reached the light and airy landing above. There, his eyes quickly settled on a painting. A gilt-framed portrait, hanging above the staircase, which showcased one of the former Earls of the Grace Hall estate: Wilfred Cecil Edward Grayson-Lawrence.

Mixed emotions fluttered through Daniel as he stared at the 4th Earl's smirking face. Oh, but he had such a strange story to tell about this gent! he mused, taking in the aristocrat's light blue eyes, sandy hair, and the dashing dark suit and white standing collar he'd been painted in.

It was a story he'd never share with anybody, mind you, not even Lacey, for fear they'd think he was deluded and/or try to force antipsychotics down his throat! But it was a story that more than explained why he'd thought, for a brief moment there, that Stevie might have been an actual, er, *medieval clergyman*, rather than a hired actor Lady Tuncaster had dressed up to represent St Nicholas...

Earl Wilfred, you see, was the first stranger-in-old-fashioned-clothing Daniel had stumbled across on the Grace Hall estate. He hadn't realised, when he'd first met the bloke – wandering the Grace Hall graveyard, just a couple of miles away – that he was a ... well, a *ghost*, to speak plainly (hence the "unsettling incidents" he kept referring to!). It was only when he found out Wilfred had died in 1913, that that spooky fact had hit home!

The second stranger Daniel had met had clearly lived in the Victorian era, and he'd found her roaming the hall itself. He glanced away from Wilfred's portrait, in the direction of the East corridor, thinking of how *she* was connected with a smaller, darker part of the house – the Nursery Wing that lay behind the fancy main bedrooms. Despite the fact she was long gone from these walls now, too – just like Wilfred – thinking of her could still make Daniel's heart ache a little...

Memories hit him all over again: the charming lilt of a French accent; the ruffles and lace of an old-fashioned white dress; long-lashed, deep brown eyes, staring up at him.

He looked at his hands for a moment, before returning his gaze to the Earl's portrait. Why he'd been able to see either of those two dearly-departed individuals, when nobody else had – not just see them, but go on to converse with them, get to know them, *feel* for them – was still a mystery to him. Although he did have a suspicion that the "gift" he'd come to realise he possessed – of being psychic – perhaps ran in his family.

Whatever the reason behind his ability to see into the hazy realm of the lingering dead, Daniel couldn't deny that the experience had been really quite unnerving at times. (To the point it had left him with a tendency to squeal and jump out of his skin anytime he heard a loud bang or after-hours footsteps wandering past the gift store – which inevitably turned out to belong to one of the cleaning team!) But he couldn't forget there'd been positives to the odd experience, too. Wilfred, in particular, had been a wise soul underneath his swaggering, hoity-toity, "*I say, old chap!*" exterior. He'd helped smooth the troubled patch Daniel and Lacey's relationship had wobbled through in that particular year, by giving out the perfect advice as to how the couple could get their love back on track. Advice Daniel, thinking of his upcoming second anniversary, knew he'd be grateful to the spook for forever.

If only, he rued, staring up at his old friend, Wilfred could give him some advice as to how to solve this *latest* hiccup in his and Lacey's marriage. But of course that was impossible. Not just because the spook was no longer in his life (Daniel had long since worked out that wandering souls remained tied to their old stomping grounds because of an unresolved issue that, once addressed, left them free to drift on to the true afterlife. Something that had happened for both the ghosts he'd known.) But because ... well, because, no matter how wise he might have been, what on earth *could* a long-dead Edwardian gent offer in the way of advice, when it came to trying for a baby that just wouldn't come?! Nothing, that's what, he realised, a touch despairingly. Apart from proposing some outlandish, old-fashioned "remedy", that involved sniffing a sage tincture or something like that, perhaps?! Daniel rued.

He'd climbed the staircase to try and find some reassurance from his old friend's image, but saw now that it had been a pointless diversion.

This time around – or, at least, until they reached the top of the notoriously-long waiting list for any sort of fertility treatment from the NHS (going private was *way* out of their budget, unfortunately, especially since they were still paying off their wedding loan) – he and Lacey were on their own with their troubles.

Which left them with just one option, Daniel reminded himself, as he tripped slowly back down to the ground floor. Like he'd thought at lunchtime, they simply had to stay as proactive as humanly possible with this fertility fight they were having. If they were to ever make the future they so badly wanted come to fruition, that was...

FOUR

Later that same day, Lacey was sitting by the fireplace in her cottage, with all the gifts she'd bought on her Christmas shopping spree with Ella laid out in front of her on the rug. She had her phone in one hand – she was updating her Christmas list as she reminded herself of what she'd bought today; the other was stroking Emme, her sweet-natured whippet, who had the softest grey fur and affectionate big black eyes. It was a peaceful moment, as they sat snuggled together by the crackling wood burner. Until, that was, the front door opened...

'Oh, hey. Did you have a nice time with Ella?' Daniel, just returned from work, tripped into the living room. Emme leapt up and dived over to greet him, tail wagging wildly; he grinned and fussed her for a moment, then sat on the sofa and kicked off his shoes.

'Brr, it's freezing out there,' he continued. 'You didn't get too cold, did you? When you were at the market? I was worried about you.'

'Oh no, I was fine. Besides, we went to the café afterwards to warm up. You should see the special hot chocolate they're doing at The Bluebird this month, Ella had one and it looked amazing! It had this adorable mini gingerbread man on top of the cream and–'

'Cream? Hot chocolate? Hang on. Why are you talking about *hot chocolate*?' Daniel suddenly looked as startled as though Lacey had just casually informed him her favourite café had started serving Amsterdam-style, cannabis-laced brownies.

She swallowed. He made a good point, actually. Why was she talking about Ella's drink?! The words had simply tumbled from her lips before she'd thought about what she was saying. Oh, dear. All these hours later, and it seemed the delicious concoction was still on her mind ... even though she'd done everything she could at the café to try and avoid looking at it!

'Um. Just because ... it looked so nice. So Christmassy, you know?' she waffled.

He frowned. 'But *you* didn't have one. Did you? Oh, Lacey – please say you didn't crack.'

'Of course I didn't! I just had a ginger tea. It was, er ... lovely.'

'Right. Right. Good. Because you know sugar might mess with your hormones. I've read *loads* about it.'

She nodded awkwardly. Yes. She was well aware of how much her husband had read up on The Potential Perils of Processed Sugar when it came to a person's fertility...

He stood up, walked over, and patted her on the shoulder, as though she was Emme and he was rewarding her good behaviour with a little positive attention. It made it hard to smile up at him, but she rallied all the same and was just about to ask him how his day had been, when he moved on to talking about dinner.

'I'll tidy this lot away then rustle something up for us,' she told him, conscious he'd been manning the gift shop all day. Not that she really felt like cooking after the busy week at work *she'd* had – although she loved her job, her role as an assistant psychologist at an eating disorders clinic certainly came with plenty of challenges. Really – she glanced longingly at her phone – she wished she could just open the oh-so-convenient food delivery app she knew was right under her fingertips, and have some scrummy takeaway brought to their front door. It was something they used to do on a fairly regular basis, especially on lazy Saturday nights when they hadn't been heading out anywhere.

Memories hit her, then. Of pizza, dripping with cheese; crispy onion bhajis; hot spring rolls with sweet-chilli dip. The images made her tummy rumble, really quite violently. Oh my goodness ... yummy!

'Lacey? Are you even listening? Did you hear what I just said?'

'What? Sorry.' She blinked up at her husband, realising thoughts of all the delicious foods that hadn't passed her lips in months had distracted her from whatever he'd just uttered.

'I said, it's OK. *I'll* make dinner. It's no problem.'

'I could at least help out–'

'No. It's fine! I'll call you when it's done.'

Lacey, recognising the determined tone to Daniel's voice, found all she could do was nod and say thanks. She supposed she should have expected he wouldn't let her into the kitchen; he never seemed to want her to set foot in that room these days. The reason being, recently, he'd taken charge of planning almost every meal she ate...

She quickly reminded herself it was kind of him to want to look after her, and that she should be grateful for his attentiveness. Especially when she thought back on their relationship: there'd been a time, you see, when they'd first moved in together, where Daniel had displayed a level of idleness she'd never encountered before, one that meant nearly every domestic-related job had fallen on her shoulders! Thankfully, her husband had finally learnt that, in the 21st century, *everyone* had to pull their weight when it came to running a household (although she'd never expected he'd end up practically kicking her out of the kitchen altogether!).

He made to walk out of the lounge, then hesitated. 'Actually. While I'm cooking – have you had a chance to do your yoga today?' He laughed awkwardly. 'I'm guessing not, since you've been out gallivanting with Ella! So, y'know ... maybe you could do a few poses while I'm in the kitchen?'

Um. *Gallivanting?* Since when had *that* quaint word entered her husband's vocabulary?! And – yoga? Lacey glanced between the crackling fire and the dark, blustery skies outside (they often left their curtains open into the evening, since they lived on a quiet lane and she liked to see the stars twinkling over the neighbouring fields). If she was honest, she felt quite tired after working all week, then being out most of the day with her best mate. If Daniel was *sure* he didn't mind rustling up a meal, then she'd really prefer just to plonk herself on the sofa and browse Netflix to find a good thriller to watch tonight!

Her reluctance to engage in any form of physical activity right at this moment in time must have shown on her face, because Daniel winced.

'Aw, Lacey, we have to be committed, remember? You *know* there're studies showing yoga can help with fertility.'

She chewed at her lip but knew she couldn't disagree with his assertion. Well, maybe there wasn't actual *scientific proof* yoga could help someone fall pregnant. But, anecdotally, the practice helped reduce stress, and certain poses were supposed to increase blood flow to a woman's ovaries and uterus. A few months ago Daniel had informed her of all these benefits; plus printed out a sheet showing exactly which postures he thought she should contort her body into on a regular basis, to help their cause. And, by regular, he meant, er ... every single day.

Which was a little different – a little more *demanding* – Lacey rued, than the once-a-week yoga classes she used to go along to with her mate from work, Charlotte.

Anyway. She noticed her husband was starting to look really quite anxious at the fact she was still sitting idly on the rug. A wash of guilt ran through her at the sight, strong enough to propel her to her feet and set out her yoga mat. Best just to keep the peace, she told herself.

And so, as Daniel went off to make dinner, she changed into her leggings then worked through a series of cobra, warrior and butterfly poses. But rather than make her feel de-stressed, with each *asana* her shoulders grew increasingly tense. Really, she'd been way more relaxed when it'd just been her and Emme lounging in the cottage! Which was a mean thought, she admitted. And yet – her husband's agitated look just now? If she was honest, it had unsettled her. Had reminded her that, before the disappointments of this year, he'd been a much cheerier character in general.

She wished he could go back to being the grinning Daniel she used to know. At the same time, she didn't blame him one little bit for the constant uneasiness that shone out of his eyes these days. She sighed and wistfully ran her hands over her flat (ish) stomach.

Right now, she was pretty sure *she* wasn't coming across as the happiest creature on earth, either...

Dinner was a healthy affair: a bowl of brown rice, topped with celery, sweetcorn and cannellini beans.

'Er. Is there any more lemon juice to sprinkle over this?' Lacey tentatively asked her husband. Because, grateful as she was for the food he'd just put on the table in front of her, one bite proved it to be really quite, um ... well, *bland*. Not that she would, in a million years, admit that to Daniel. Besides, it wasn't his fault. He was a great cook but, since he'd read that oil was basically a processed food (and so a no-no when it came to making their bodies the healthiest they could be for their fertility battle), he'd decided, for now, to ban it from their kitchen cupboards. He was definitely still finding his feet, though, when it came to filling the flavour-gap the absence of a good glug of extra virgin olive oil left behind!

'Of course there is.' He seemed really happy by her request, and jumped up to fetch some fresh lemon slices from the fridge. 'Here you go. You can never go wrong with some extra vitamin C!'

She felt a little better as he smiled approvingly at her. Until, that was, she found out there was no dessert on offer ... which was disappointing because, despite clearing her plate, she didn't feel remotely full. Oh, well. Maybe she could grab a banana later on. She knew that was a Daniel-approved snack.

After washing up the dishes, she made them both a mug of mint tea then wandered through to join her husband in the living room. When she got there she realised their Christmas tree lights hadn't yet been switched on, so she made sure to do that before she joined him on the sofa.

'That's a bit cheerier!' she smiled, with a nod at their pretty tree, which was decorated in co-ordinating shades of gold and pale blue. Not that *she* could take any credit for how chic it looked. Oh no. Left to her, the thing would've been draped with clashing colours of tinsel and topped with a lopsided angel! Thankfully, Daniel was a lot more creative than she was. He had quite the talent when it came to anything interiors-related, you see, and had taken a lot of time to find the *perfect* Christmas decorations for their home. Not, she thought sadly, that he'd seemed half as happy setting everything up this year, as he had twelve months ago...

She glanced at him, and noticed he was looking at the tree, too. Only, there was a look on his face that made her tummy twist. A look of ... was that regret? she fretted.

Before she could ask if he was OK, though, something on the flickering TV caught his attention. A theme tune, to a show that was just starting.

'Look, Lace. It's *How Babies are Born*. We missed it last week. Let's see what happens in this episode!'

Oh. Right. Her heart sank. Because – well the clue was in the title, of course. But *How Babies are Born* was a weekly TV show, that followed all the drama of women giving birth on a real-life maternity ward. A tad different from the stylish Netflix thriller she'd been hoping to settle down to watch tonight.

Daniel must have sensed her hesitation for the second time that evening at one of his suggestions, because he turned to her and wrung his hands.

'It's important we watch stuff like this, don't you think? Because this'll be us before we know it! I'm sure it will. Definitely.' He nodded so vigorously, his dishevelled dark hair bounced up and down. 'So it'll help us know what to expect!'

'Yes. True. But–'

'Please don't say "but". We have to stay positive, remember?! We're doing all the right things.' His eyes turned a little wild as he put those points to her. 'Plus, you haven't forgotten what the doctor said, have you?'

No. No, of course she hadn't. How could she forget the appointments they'd had with their GP recently? They hadn't exactly been pleasant, after all. Not for her, at least.

After a year of trying unsuccessfully for their own little one, you see, they'd been entitled to some preliminary fertility investigations on the NHS. All their tests – including an internal ultrasound that she'd had to go to the local hospital to have just the other week, and had been über-nervous about (and which, actually, had turned out to be nothing to worry about – a lot less uncomfortable than a smear test!) had come back showing nothing of concern.

Which was great news! their GP, Dr Rhines, had told them. Of course, they were still entitled to see a specialist ... not that they should expect an appointment any time soon, she'd warned, given the current NHS waiting times. But, for now, their test results meant she could class their infertility as "unexplained"; and she saw no reason why, given they were in the under-35 age bracket, that with a little more time and trying – and a healthy lifestyle and low stress levels, she added – a baby would eventually materialise.

Eventually materialise? Daniel had been left really quite upbeat by that phrase, Lacey recalled. In fact, he'd left the appointment determined that "unexplained" meant they simply had to try harder in their quest to have a family of their own.

For her, though, the term "unexplained" had left her rattled. Because if there'd been a definite problem found as to why they weren't falling pregnant, perhaps some medication or medical procedure could've conclusively righted the issue. "Unexplained", while of course hopeful in some senses, also felt vague and open-ended. Like there *were* no particular answers. Just more uncertainty – at least until a fertility specialist decided on what they should do next.

As for her husband's assertion their test results simply meant they had to fight harder to get what they wanted? Hm. She thought back over the past year, of all the things that had become a part of her life since they'd begun their pregnancy journey. Not just the homemade, oil-free meals and relentless yoga sessions. But the ovulation test strips she paid a small fortune for, then squinted over the results of, every single month. The daily questions a fertility app on her phone asked her about her bodily sensations: was she experiencing vaginal itching; crying spells; constipation?! (She still didn't quite understand the reason for the ridiculously-intimate enquiries — maybe she was missing the point, but it never seemed to add up to meaning anything??). The course of acupuncture Daniel had pleaded with her to have through the summer. (She didn't know what good that had done, either, because her nervousness of needles meant every session had left her with nothing more than wobbly legs and a squeamish feeling in her tummy!). The omega 3 supplements, the organic skincare range she'd swapped over to using, Daniel's suggestion she retreat to bed an hour earlier each night than she used to, to cram more sleep into her routine...

The point she was trying to make was — was it even possible for them to spend *more time* than they already had, these past months? Exploring and putting into practice things they could do to make their bodies more amenable to creating a child...?

Just as Lacey was anxiously pondering that question, her attention was caught by the TV programme playing in front of her. A woman in her mid-thirties, who already had four children, was being rushed onto the ward to deliver her fifth, laughing (yes, laughing?!) in between her contractions as she joked about "how fast this one was going to come out!".

Five babies? This woman had the privilege of *five* babies? How was that fair, when she and Daniel couldn't even seem to manage one?!

A yucky sense of bitterness, of jealousy stole into Lacey's heart. It wasn't something she was proud of. She knew it wasn't a kind way to feel. And it *definitely* – she glanced at the sparkly white angel on top of their twinkling tree – was not the sort of emotion that summed up the spirit of the Christmas season.

She couldn't help it, though. She'd *known* this programme would make her feel all-sorts-of-unsettled. That was why she hadn't wanted to watch it in the first place. She was quite sure the other, estimated, one-in-seven couples in the UK that were going through similar fertility battles would feel exactly the same, she rued. At least, though, she wouldn't have to sit through another episode next weekend. She thought of seeing Rose today, and her grandma's mention of F-Group, and nodded. Yes. Strange as it might sound, courtesy of her mum and her grandma's feminist group, they had plans for next Saturday night that were going to be much more festive than sitting at home, watching TV. Plans that would hopefully be a great distraction from their troubles, into the bargain.

For now, though – not wanting to make Daniel any more on edge than she already inadvertently had this evening – Lacey fell quiet and continued watching the drama unfolding in front of her. In the birthing suite, just as the mother had predicted, Baby No. 5 began crowning. A couple of pushes later, he – a sweet little boy – slipped into the world. He let out a big hearty cry, and the mum and dad immediately had tears in their eyes.

Lacey felt herself welling up, too. Not just because the baby looked so cute and adorable, though, or because of the miracle-of-life she'd just witnessed. It also wasn't solely because her arms felt cold and empty, compared to the woman on screen who was now nestling her newborn next to her chest.

It was because, well...

She took in the way the dad on the screen was glowing with pride as he surveyed his partner and their brand new baby. And then her gaze slid to Daniel and her sense of tearfulness grew as she thought of how *her* husband never looked at her with anything even *close* to pride these days. Instead, every month now, as all their trying came to nothing, she had to brace herself to give him news of yet another negative pregnancy test, then swallow down the disappointment in his eyes.

It wasn't nice. She hated that she couldn't give him what she knew he needed to be happy. But, more than that, she felt ashamed.

Her thoughts drifted, once more, to last year. To when she'd thought being a mother was something that couldn't happen for her, because of those unaddressed demons from her past.

Although she'd finally – and successfully – faced those demons, the process had taken time. And during that time she'd treated her husband badly. Well, not *badly*, exactly. But she hadn't been open or truthful with him about her feelings. Had, instead, batted away every single one of his – very natural – attempts to talk about when might be the right time to start a family of their own, something he'd personally felt ready for since they'd come home from their honeymoon.

Although she hadn't meant to make him suffer, Lacey knew her doubts, and her avoidance of that important conversation for so long, had caused her husband angst and worry. Not only that – all those months she'd spent fighting against the idea of motherhood, was time that could have been spent differently.

If she'd taken her husband's lead and been more agreeable to starting their fertility journey earlier, perhaps they wouldn't be in the tough spot they were in now. Because one of those months she'd wasted ... well, maybe not wasted, exactly, because she *had* needed to sort her head out ... but one of those months might have boasted the perfect conditions for conception. They might indeed have had a child of their own by this Christmas, if she hadn't evaded poor Daniel's pleading for so long, last year!

That thought was so overwhelming – and guilt-inducing – that a big lump grew in Lacey's throat.

And then she thought of her dubiousness when it came to her husband's determination to "try harder" with their fertility challenge. The temptation she'd felt around Ella's hot chocolate earlier. Her lack of motivation around her daily yoga practice this evening.

What was she doing?! she chided herself. Yes, she might be a little jaded from a year of disappointments; but that was no excuse to start slacking on, or doubting, any of the lifestyle adjustments her beautiful husband – and even their GP – thought might make the difference between their conceiving or not! It just wasn't.

Daniel was right. They had to stay positive. They had to keep fighting. Not just because her insides craved and ached to have a little Lina all of her own.

But because giving this battle her all was the very least she owed her husband, after her behaviour of last year...

FIVE

The next morning, Daniel woke early. He glanced towards the window, where the cool light of the winter's morning was gently filtering in at the edges of the curtains. He could tell it was cold outside; icy, perhaps, judging by how still the day felt. A complete contrast to how toasty *he* was, tucked under the duvet with Lacey still dozing next to him.

Despite that, he was keen to get up. He knew why. It was to do with the programme he'd watched on TV last night, *How Babies are Born*. If he was honest, seeing all those couples welcoming their precious bundles of joy into the world had left him a little edgy by the time he'd gone to bed. Ever-so-slightly jealous, too. But before he'd drifted off to sleep he'd tried to push those unhelpful feelings aside. Had reflected, instead, on what he'd uttered, really quite insistently to Lacey at the start of the programme: they had to stay positive that they themselves would be joining the ranks of those parents before long, especially when you considered what their GP had said at their last appointment. Of course, Dr Rhines was no specialist in the area, but given that all the tests they'd had so far were normal, their infertility was being classed, for now, as "unexplained".

Which was good news, wasn't it? Daniel reminded himself. He'd found it reassuring to know that nothing overtly sinister seemed to be wrong with the way their bodies were functioning. In fact, he'd taken the findings to mean the outcome of their fertility journey was probably in their own hands; which, he supposed, was why the doctor had reminded them to keep up a healthy lifestyle!

Anyway. Reminding himself of Dr Rhines' words – combined with the sense of yearning all those adorable babies' faces had once again triggered in him last night – meant he'd woken rejuvenated in his resolve, to do whatever it took for him and Lacey to eventually have a little one of their own. Or, at least, everything they could do outside of receiving some definitive fertility treatment, like ovulation drugs or even full-blown IVF – because until their appointment with an NHS consultant came through, those options weren't on the table for now. (Although honestly, if he had the money, he'd already be booked in at a swanky private fertility clinic somewhere – really, it was pretty sad how unsupported people experiencing trouble conceiving were in the UK, something he'd never realised before.)

He shrugged on a hoodie and some tracksuit bottoms, then headed downstairs, to where a bleary-eyed Emme welcomed him, her tail thudding gently against the soft blankets of her fleecy bed. He gave her a pat ... then looked around the kitchen, lifted his chin and walked determinedly to the fridge.

A short time later, he headed back upstairs. Only, this time, he had a loaded tray clasped in his hands, which he set down on the bed.

'Lacey? Morning, sleepy head.'

He smiled as his wife blinked up at him. She looked early-morning cute, with her dark blonde hair sprawled all over her pillow. So cute, he felt a stir of longing, and was almost tempted to slide back under the duvet with her...

Except, what would be the point? It was too early in her cycle for her to be ovulating, after all. Funny he knew stuff like that now, he rued. If he was honest, once upon a time women's menstrual cycles had been nothing but a slightly-scary mystery to him: aside from having to run out and panic-buy pain killers when Lacey's monthly cramps struck harder than usual, he'd always been happy to stay in the dark when it came to whatever-was-going-on with her hormones. Which had probably been a bit immature of him, he supposed.

He wasn't like that now, though! When a baby hadn't come after their first few months of trying, he'd set about studying the female reproductive cycle as intensely as though he'd decided to take up a career in gynaecology. Now, he knew all about luteal phases and LH surges, hah!

Not that that "insider knowledge" as to the mechanics of his wife's uterus seemed to have helped much in their quest for a little one, of course...

Hm. Daniel realised, then, that his thoughts about wombs and womanly matters had effectively cooled any sense of lust he'd had towards Lacey just now! He shrugged resignedly and drew back the curtains instead. Outside, just as he'd suspected, the front yard – and the rolling fields beyond – were covered with an icing-sugar-like dusting of early frost.

'Morning. What time is it? It feels early,' his wife yawned.

'Don't worry about that.' He wouldn't be waking her unless he knew she'd had time to have a full eight hours of slumber. Good sleep was so important to regulating fertility hormones, after all! Accordingly, 'Did you sleep well?' he checked.

'Yes. Yes, I did, thanks.'

'Good. Don't forget to log that in your app. Also,' he smiled eagerly, 'I've brought you breakfast.'

'You have? Oh, Daniel, you didn't need to do that...'

She trailed off, a little frown appearing on her face as she looked at the tray next to her. So he quickly explained *what* he'd prepared – with the fresh sense of purpose he'd woken with, you see, he'd decided to whip up a super-food breakfast. What better way to continue cramming nutrients into their bodies?!

And so, there was a glass of bright green smoothie, containing celery, cucumber and raw kale. Quinoa porridge topped with almond milk, milled flaxseed and goji berries. A special herbal tea his mum had found at a health food store, which would supposedly help balance Lacey's hormones thanks to the mix of raspberry leaf, spearmint, nettle and red clover it contained.

Finally, there was also a pot of supplements on the tray, alongside a glass of water for his wife to wash them down with. As he surveyed the array of different-sized-and-coloured pills on offer, Daniel couldn't help but remember that, when they'd first started out on their baby-making venture, Lacey had only taken a grand total of *two* tablets to support their attempts to conceive: the über-important folic acid, plus vitamin D. But then, as the months had passed, he'd wondered if there might be more supplements that could help their failing quest. Sure enough – lots of time on Google later – and he'd discovered a whole army of products he'd never heard of before, that were meant to boost a person's fertility: Coenzyme Q10, acetyl l-carnitine, selenium, acai berry extract, chasteberry, to name a few. It was an expensive venture, but he'd set about buying everything he could get his hands on. It meant one of their kitchen cupboards now looked like a shelving unit from Holland & Barrett; and that they now *both* choked back a *handful* of pills on a daily basis. (He knew he had to do his bit, too, when it came to being in the healthiest form of his life, so he could – hopefully – create super-sperm!!)

The day they finally fell pregnant though, he nodded firmly, all of this effort and expense would prove worth it. Speaking of which–

As he gazed again at the fields outside their bedroom window, he thought of how he loved to run in the countryside several times a week. Always had done. But, ever since Dr Rhines had told them to keep up a healthy lifestyle, he'd considered those runs an even more important part of his schedule. Having a great diet was one thing, after all; but for maximum good health, a person also had to exercise regularly. Right?

It was that thought that got him considering whether or not *Lacey* was really doing enough activity each week, in order to optimise her health from that angle? She did love walking, he acknowledged. Especially if it involved a dog! Not just Emme, but also the canines at Sunny Side, an animal rescue centre she volunteered at. She also did a few yoga poses each day. But those pursuits never got her remotely out of breath – so did they really count as *proper* exercise? Daniel wondered. She *had* done kickboxing for a bit last year, with her mum, but had long since packed that in because she'd found it too heavy-going for her liking (it was fair to say she'd never been a big fan of over-exerting herself on the physical front!).

Perhaps that needed to change, he mused. Perhaps she needed to start doing something more cardio-based. Something that would really get her heart rate up and boost her circulation, her fitness. Because that could possibly help her fertility too, couldn't it? Thanks to the, er, improved blood flow and feel-good hormones it would stimulate??

Hm. As his wife sat up in bed to eat her bowl of quinoa, Daniel – motivated by the determined state of mind he'd woken with – grabbed his phone from his bedside table and quickly checked out his theory. Sure enough, it wasn't hard to find articles online which linked the endorphin-stimulating benefits of aerobic exercise to an improved fertile status (although, granted, they did warn that you shouldn't over-do it.)

Well, that settled things, he nodded. Lacey *had* to get moving more!

The only question was – how to make that happen? He often had to encourage her just to do her yoga, after all, and that only involved a few easy-peasy stretches!

He looked at the fields again. And that was when he was hit with an idea…

'Once you're done with breakfast, let's head out for an – *ahem* – walk, together. A good *long walk*, I mean,' he proposed slyly.

Lacey glanced at the window. He saw a flicker of doubt cross her face, presumably because of the frosty scene outside.

'A *long* walk?' she checked, her tone dubious. 'But – we're going to your mum's later, aren't we?'

'It's only early!' he encouraged. 'If we set off soon, we'll have plenty of time.'

Still, she hesitated. Her eyes flickered back to the lovely warm duvet she was still snugly swathed in, something that made him feel a beat of both panic *and* irritation. Didn't she *want* a baby? Didn't she want to put the effort in to making that happen? To follow Dr Rhines' advice to live a healthy lifestyle … in *every way possible*?! He got that it was a cold morning. In the past he, too, would've loved to have stayed under that thick cosy duvet and have a lovely, well-deserved lie-in. But they had a fight on their hands, and a baby wouldn't come their way by just lounging in bed all day! (Well, ideally it *would* have done, hah. But not, it seemed, in their case…)

'OK. Sounds great. Give me five minutes to get ready!'

Oh. Daniel blinked in surprise as he realised Lacey was getting out of bed, without any further coaxing on his part. Actually, she was scrambling out of bed, with an earnest smile on her face.

Well. *Great*, he nodded, gratified by her unexpected enthusiasm. In fact, a little smile played on his lips as he realised Part One of his spur-of-the-moment plan to boost her fitness was playing out more smoothly than he'd hoped. It meant, once they were out in the depths of the countryside, it would be easy to spring Part Two on his unsuspecting wife…!

A short time later, he, Lacey, and Emme found themselves heading down the icy country lane outside their terraced cottage.

'Brr. It's bitter this morning, isn't it?' Lacey commented. 'Not just bitter – absolutely flipping freezing! I'm shivering already.'

Daniel turned to her, surprised. Yes, it was a typically-nippy December morning. But he wouldn't have expected his wife to be *shivering*, not given all the gear – after thoughts of being worried about her catching a chill at the Christmas market yesterday – he'd encouraged her to don: two pairs of thick socks, a big woolly hat, a pair of his thermal running gloves, plus, of course, her chunky black parka jacket.

He hesitated, wondering if they should turn back. But then he thought of his sneaky plan to slip more exercise into her life: he didn't want to delay in putting that into action! So he rubbed her shoulders and suggested they walk a little faster.

'That should get you warmed up,' he said firmly.

Thankfully, his suggestion they up their pace seemed to do the trick. With Lacey more comfortable, they continued down the lane for quite a while, enjoying the seasonal views of trees dappled with frost. They even saw a cute red-breasted robin, pilfering red berries from the winter bushes lining the roadside!

But simply walking with a bit more purpose, Daniel knew, wasn't going to provide the heart-pumping health benefits he wanted for his wife. So after they'd climbed a stile to join a track that wove around the fields, he knew it was the perfect time to put Part 2 of his *Get Lacey Moving!* plan into action.

He unclipped Emme from her leash, so she could run free for a while. Then he began striding forward. The frozen grass crunched under his feet. Step after step he pushed on, knowing that, with his longer legs, he'd easily cover more ground than Lacey. If she wanted to keep up, he nodded ... she'd have to *really* put some effort in.

Sure enough, after a few minutes, Daniel heard his wife's breathing start to quicken. Result! Emboldened, he increased his pace again. And then they turned a corner, and suddenly the terrain became quite muddy, and veered uphill, into the bargain.

Lacey's breathing became distinctly wheezy as they headed along the incline.

'D ... Daniel? Can we–' *huff, puff* '–slow down a ... a bit?'

Slow down? Er, no! They were just getting started, he thought resolutely.

'Keep going! This is good for you! You're doing really well. Stay with me!' he encouraged. He stomped on, moving so quickly now, that to keep with him Lacey was forced to break into a jog – just like he'd hoped would happen!

Now her heart rate would be surging, he smiled to himself.

It was only when he reached the top of the field that Daniel finally came to a stop. He turned around, ready to cheer his wife's efforts once more. But what he saw behind him made his heart wobble with unexpected sympathy.

Oh.

Lacey was tripping towards him, gasping for breath. Her cheeks were bright red and there was sweat glistening on her forehead. She'd ripped off her hat and gloves and unzipped her jacket, too, clearly no longer feeling the cold of the day after her exertion!

'I feel a bit dizzy,' she gulped.

She reached for his arm and he supported her while she caught her breath. He was hit with a pang of guilt as he listened to her noisy panting: had he pushed her too hard? Only, if she was in better shape, she wouldn't have ended up in this kind of sweaty mess just from a little bit of – admittedly uphill – jogging, would she?! So, really, he thought, his sympathy flipping to skittishness, this was simply proof his wife *did* need to start working harder on her overall fitness.

'Babe! Did you realise you were in such bad shape?' he cringed, when her breathing finally settled down.

She let go of his arm and laughed uncertainly. 'Um. Well I've never been much of a runner, have I?'

'That was more of a shuffle than a run!' he exclaimed.

Her cheeks grew red again. 'We *were* going uphill, though,' she protested, gently.

A fresh sense of panic started to claw at Daniel. Why was she being awkward about this, instead of admitting what the sweat around her hairline was evidence of? She was unfit. Period. And that wasn't healthy.

'You remember what the doctor said? That we have to keep up a healthy lifestyle? Well–' he waved his arms around, fretting that what he was about to say might be true '–I never thought about it until today, but you ... you being unfit could be stopping us from getting pregnant! So you need to work harder on that, Lacey. I mean, I run all the time! It's not fair you do nothing more than stroll around with Emme.'

The words burst out of him. Immediately afterwards, he bit his lip, realising he'd sounded harsher than he'd meant to. Even he knew it was doubtful *the sole reason* they weren't conceiving, would be due to his wife not regularly whizzing around the fields in a pair of running tights.

At the same time ... *something* was stopping a baby from happening, so they couldn't be lax. Any weak areas had to be addressed, and quickly, because he felt, by this point, like he'd been waiting to be a dad since forever!

Lacey dropped her eyes to the ground. Daniel's heart thudded with a weird mix of angst and anxiety as he waited for her to say something. When she finally looked back at him her eyes were damp.

'I'm sorry,' she gulped. 'I ... I didn't realise. I thought ... I do a lot of walking, don't I? Not just with Emme. I walk the dogs at Sunny Side, too. And then there's my yoga. I thought that was enough.'

'You do try,' he agreed. 'But, clearly, you need to do more! We *both* have to keep doing everything we can. All these little changes to our lifestyle ... you don't know which one might make the difference. I've read loads of stories about couples falling pregnant after they kicked sugar or started taking selenium tablets or whatever. For us, it might be you getting fitter! It's worth trying, right?'

She nodded, quickly. 'I agree. Sorry. I'll make more of an effort. I promise.'

She looked ashamed, then, and it made him want to hug her, to pull her close and tell her that everything would be OK.

But he didn't ... because he *couldn't* say that. All he could do was hope, he sighed. Hope that fighting – to be in perfect health, in perfect shape, and to have a perfect mind set, *at all times* – would help them finally achieve their dream of a family of their own.

*

At lunchtime – after Lacey had taken a shower to wash away all the sweat she'd worked up – Daniel clicked open his car and they headed across town to his mum's house. When they arrived on her street, however, he felt edgy all over again. Because one glance, you see, told him he wouldn't be able to park on his mum's driveway, the way he was used to doing.

Not when his usual parking slot had been nabbed by another car.

A little red Skoda, that he saw nearly every day of the working week, too. The reason being, that that was *Neville's* car.

Yes. Neville – as in his boss at Grace Hall.

He let out a long exhale as he instead manoeuvred into a spot on the roadside. The sound caused Lacey to snap her head towards him.

'Everything OK?' she frowned.

'Yeah. I'm fine. It's just–' Daniel waved impatiently at his boss's car '–he's here all the time, these days!'

She hesitated, before reaching out to squeeze his knee. 'I know. And that must be strange for you. But ... at least you don't have to worry about your mum being lonely anymore.'

That was true, Daniel had to concede. As he got out of the car he thought of how his mum, Hazel – a widow for many years, because of his dad sadly passing from cancer while he'd been only a kid – had spent a huge chunk of her life without a partner. That had all changed when, last October, at a Halloween party at Grace Hall (held by Lady Tuncaster to raise funds for the roof repairs her home had desperately needed) she and Neville had become ... well, *acquainted*, was the word, Daniel supposed.

He had a flashback to the moment they'd first set eyes on one another, in the grounds of the old hall. To how his mum had gone on to spend the rest of the evening twirling around the dance floor in his boss's arms, before they'd shyly swapped phone numbers at the end of the night.

Although he'd felt slightly awkward, initially, at seeing his mum giggling and fluttering her eyelashes in Neville's direction, Daniel recalled he'd been in a great mood that night, and had generously decided his ever-so-jolly boss and his been-alone-too-long mum would be a sweet fit, should they decide to get to know one another better after the party.

Now, though, just over a year later ... he wasn't feeling quite so magnanimous towards the situation. The reason being, he hadn't really thought through what it might *mean*, if the pair became a proper couple, the way – after month on month of tearoom get-togethers, trips to museums, and even a summer break to the Isle of Wight to visit Osborne House – they'd become...

'Darlings! Lovely to see you.' As they headed down the driveway, Hazel suddenly appeared at her front door. Her frizzy curls were brushed out and bouncing around her pink cheeks, and she was wearing a cheery Christmas-tree-print apron over her skirt and cable-knit cardigan. She waved urgently at them as they approached. 'Come in, quickly now. I've got the fire on. Jesus knows, it's too cold to loiter outside today.'

'It *is* cold,' Lacey agreed, greeting her mother-in-law with a kiss on the cheek.

'Oh, your nose is freezing!' Hazel giggled. 'Poor dear.' She turned to Daniel next, gave him a big hug, then they all headed for the toasty living room.

When they got there, the first thing Daniel saw was Neville, sitting on the sofa in a fleece top and blue jeans. He had a newspaper on his lap and ... well, his shoes must have been in the hall (or even upstairs, Daniel winced, knowing the guy regularly stayed the night these days) because his feet were clad only in socks.

Blue-'n-black striped socks, which should've been inoffensive ... but which Daniel couldn't help but eyeball in a fit of annoyance. Given he'd been at work yesterday, today was the start of his weekend; and he really didn't want to spend his time off hanging out with his boss and his flipping stripy socks! Especially when they gave the bloke such an *at home* vibe, one he was finding it harder and harder to come to terms with.

Not, Daniel had to admit, that a pair of socks was the worst thing he'd caught the guy wearing on one of these out-of-work encounters... One day, in the summer, he'd popped round to see his mum – only to find Neville, barbequing in the back yard in a pair of ... of really *quite revealing* chino shorts that had reached barely half-way down his thigh! Even now, the memory of his boss, grinning in his childhood garden, with his pale, hairy legs on show, made him cringe to his bones.

Not that he wanted to be mean. In fact, as Neville jumped off the sofa to greet him and Lacey with a hearty handshake and a big, jolly smile, a part of him felt bad for being anything but welcoming towards his boss. Neville, after all, was a kind-hearted man. Amiable. Gentle. His mum was in good hands with him. Daniel knew he should just be happy for her, that she'd stumbled into this second shot at love, courtesy of his job at Grace Hall. And he *was*, deep down. It was just ... well–

His eyes flit to one of his favourite photos of him and his late dad, Henry, that his mum kept on the lounge windowsill. It showed them laughing together as they played football at a nearby park. The image might have been caught a long, *long* time ago – he'd only been nine when his dad had died. And most people might think it didn't feature a particularly memorable occasion. Having a kick-around? Kids did that with their parents all the time, some might shrug. What could be so special about *that*? For him, though ... he still remembered that particular day like it was yesterday. He ... he'd joined his school's football team, you see, and his dad had been really proud and wanted to help him train. That had been their first session together – his dad had set up drills to help him learn dribbling techniques. His mum had come along to watch, hence the photo. She'd also mock-scolded them at the end of the afternoon, for how muddy they'd gotten, he recalled wryly.

Daniel hadn't cared about the mud in his eyes or splattered all over his new football boots, though. He'd just felt excited and carefree, like any little boy in the world would, to be running around in the fresh air with one of his favourite people in the world!

Neither of them had known, then, that their time together was soon to come to an abrupt end...

Oh. A lump grew in Daniel's throat. In fact, he found himself swallowing back an unexpected sob. He still missed his dad. Still wondered, what life would've been like if that stupid cancer hadn't come along and robbed him of all the years he *should've* had, to share with his family.

His eyes flickered back to Neville, who was now chatting on the sofa to Lacey. Perhaps, he sighed, given what had happened with his dad, he could be forgiven for finding it difficult, sometimes, to have another man in his childhood home.

His brooding thoughts were interrupted by his mum – who'd gone off to fetch them all a cup of hot tea – bustling back into the room with a tray of mugs.

'I've a special treat for you, too,' she beamed, setting her tray on the coffee table and nodding at a plate of biscuits it also contained. 'I've been experimenting. I baked these cookies especially for you two, just this morning! The lady at the health food shop suggested I use unsweetened applesauce, to replace the sugar. Let's hope they taste OK!'

They certainly *smelt* good, Daniel thought, breathing in the delicious scent of allspice and cinnamon – flavours, his mum explained, she'd specifically used because she wanted the biscuits to taste "Christmassy".

It turned out they tasted better than OK. They tasted *good*, full of oats and applesauce and raisins. So good, that Daniel's mood perked up, helped, too by his mum's thoughtfulness in supporting his and Lacey's clean eating plan. (She was definitely keen to get a grandchild into her life, he knew, thinking wryly of the "fertility tea" she'd also bought Lacey from the health food store, the one he'd brewed for his wife this very morning.)

They all ate the scrummy cookies and drank decaffeinated tea and chatted. The fire roared on, tinsel glistened on the Christmas tree in the corner, and Daniel realised his mum looked brighter than she'd done at any point over the last few years (apart, if he was honest, from the day of his wedding to Lacey – she'd been overjoyed to be a mother-of-the-groom!). Perhaps, he thought a little shamefacedly, he'd er, *overreacted* a bit to Neville's presence today. The guy didn't mean any harm, did he? Far from it – he just wanted to make Hazel happy.

But just as Daniel's uneasy mood was beginning to melt away ... his mum dropped an unexpected announcement into the mix.

'Darlings, I want to let you know something – Neville is going to be spending Christmas Day here this year. Won't that be lovely?'

As his mum and his boss shared a fond look, Daniel blinked. What? That wasn't news he'd been expecting to hear. Although he supposed it made sense: Neville didn't have any other family or children of his own, so who was he *supposed* to spend the holiday with? At the same time – and even though he knew he was being pretty miserly to think this way – he immediately felt put out by his mum's declaration. Ever since he and Lacey had started dating they'd split their time on Christmas Day between her mum's house, and his. This year, they were supposed to be having their Christmas lunch here at Hazel's, then going on to Sadie's for drinks and nibbles in the evening. But Daniel couldn't really imagine having *his boss* sitting at the dining table with them, as they laughed and pulled crackers and his mum got tipsy on something sparkling! And they would be exchanging presents, too, of course – did that mean he had to buy something for Neville, now?!

For his mum's sake, he tried not to cringe as the feeling his boss was intruding too much into his personal life made a furious return. He couldn't pretend to be overly-happy about her news either, though, so after throwing her a half-smile he left the trio to talk amongst themselves and, instead, picked up his phone. He flicked idly through Facebook, hoping to distract himself from his fresh tetchiness about Neville. What he discovered on his screen, though, didn't do anything to improve his mood: the reason being, he found himself suddenly staring at *the* most adorable photo, uploaded by his best mate Rob that morning...

Daniel took in the scene. On one side of the photo was Rob, and on the other, his petite, sweet partner Abby. They were both holding hands with their son, the gorgeous little Milo, who, at fifteen months old, was the cutest toddler imaginable, given his neat dark hair, big expressive eyes and heart-melting giggle! The little boy was dressed in a pair of mini jeans and a Christmas jumper with Rudolph on the front, an appropriate outfit given it looked – from the elves and the snow-covered cabin in the background of the photo – that they were visiting a Santa's Grotto somewhere.

Milo's first time meeting Santa Claus, at the Mulberry Garden Centre, Rob had written above the image. *Followed by hot chocolates all round in the café. Happy holidays everyone!*

He couldn't help it. A flash of hot envy hit Daniel hard. Especially when he thought of how Milo – who he absolutely loved to visit and fuss over and play tractors 'n diggers with, every chance he got! – had been the result of an *unplanned* pregnancy. Yes, that was right – Rob and Abby had only been together a couple of months or so before being blessed with the news they were expecting a baby they *hadn't even had to try for*. How was that fair?! Daniel thought glumly, as he reflected his mate's experience of starting a family against the over-twelve-months-of-negative-pregnancy-tests he and Lacey had gone through.

Not that he wasn't happy for Rob. He wasn't *that* awful a person. He loved seeing what a happy little family he, Abby and Milo made.

He just ... well, he just didn't understand why a little one wasn't happening for him and Lacey. He just didn't. And some days he honestly felt like his head could almost explode with the worry of it all!

Anyway. He was just giving his mate's photo a thumbs up, when he realised his mum had stopped talking about the Christmas floral arrangements she was helping put together for her local church, St Bede's ("Marjory wants to be terribly chic and do an ivory-theme with pure white roses and lilies, but *I* think sticking with classic red 'n green will be so much merrier!"), and was, instead, tapping him on the leg.

'Daniel, did you hear what I just said? I was asking if you've anything nice planned for you and Lacey's second wedding anniversary? It's just around the corner now, isn't it? Unless, of course,' she twinkled at Lacey, 'he doesn't want to say. He might have a lovely surprise planned for you!' she told her daughter-in-law.

Lacey, on the sofa next to Neville, sent an uncertain smile his way. He wasn't surprised by that: maybe she sensed he hadn't even bought so much as a card for her yet, never mind have a "lovely surprise" planned. Not because he didn't want to celebrate the milestone. Of course he did – their wedding had been one of the most special days in his life. But, if he was honest, being reminded they were now *two years* into their marriage without so much as a peep of a fertilised egg travelling down his wife's fallopian tubes, made him feel more disturbed than delighted!

SIX

Monday found Lacey back at work, walking through the corridors of The Serenity Clinic. The eating disorders centre was housed in a white-fronted Georgian building in the city of York itself, and treated outpatients dealing with a number of issues related to food. Now they'd headed into the month of December, though, there was a *particular* topic the centre always made sure to address: namely, the intense focus around food and eating that came with the festive season, and how it might affect their clients' progress.

It was a serious topic; so much so, even now, with years of experience in her role as an assistant psychologist under her belt, Lacey fretted over the potential of the Christmas period to cause setbacks in her patients' precious recoveries. She hated the anxiety she'd begin to see etched on their faces, caused from over-exposure to all the food-related adverts – whether on TV or social media or in the press – the winter months inevitably brought into their lives. Adverts that, for most people of course, were happy and fun: they usually showed families drooling over tables crammed to the hilt with festive fare, like stuffing and mashed potatoes, jugs of gravy and bread sauce, steaming apple pies and Christmas puddings. But that scenario was one many of her clients – dependant on their faith or background – dreaded having to face, come December 25th.

Of course, most of the population couldn't even *imagine* having a problem sitting down to a Christmas meal, Lacey knew. If you didn't have an eating disorder, a big part of the holiday season was the joy of indulgence, of sharing food with family and friends. Just like the shoppers at the Christmas market on Saturday had been doing, she mused wistfully, recalling the blissful looks she'd witnessed around her as people had devoured the sweet crêpes and sugar donuts and hot mince pies the food stalls had been offering. Treat foods – since working with eating-disordered-patients and seeing it wasn't a luxury everyone enjoyed – she'd come to appreciate she herself had a healthy balance with.

Or, at least, she ... she *used* to have a healthy balance with those kinds of foods, Lacey rued.

Now ... well. Thoughts of the brown-rice-and-endless-varieties-of-green-vegetables diet Daniel was determined they needed to follow these days flit through her mind.

But that was a whole different story, she quickly nodded, before glancing down at the stack of handbooks she was carrying. They were titled "Tips for Dealing with the Holiday Season", and they reminded her she had an important job to focus on this morning. One that, ironically, not even her currently-rumbling tummy (thanks to the breakfast her husband had barged downstairs to prepare before she left the house earlier, being made up of nothing more than a few chunks of grapefruit and a sprinkling of sunflower seeds) should distract her from. Namely, she was running the first in a series of special workshops The Serenity Clinic held every December, to help their clients through the Christmas period – aptly called their "Holiday Season Support Group".

Speaking of which ... she'd almost reached the group therapy room at the back of the building, where she knew her clients would already be waiting for her. Before she could push open the double doors and get started on the session, though, she heard her phone ping in her pocket.

She should put that on silent, Lacey realised, pulling it free. But, first, she checked the message.

Oh. It was from Daniel.

Of course it was from Daniel. Because it was his day off today, wasn't it? she reminded herself. He always got a day off in the week when he'd worked at the gift shop on a Saturday. Which meant...

She bit her lip, knowing, from experience, *exactly* what that meant ... that he had hours of free time on his hands, time he seemed to like to use, these days, to fret over her.

She went on to read what he'd written.

Remember not to work too hard today! I know you get worried about your patients at Christmas time, but you've got to focus on US this year, ok?

Lacey, thinking of how much supporting every single one of her clients meant to her, almost felt a beat of annoyance at his teetering-on-bossy words. But then she thought back to Saturday night. To the guilt she'd been hit with, when she reflected on her hesitation, last year, around the whole motherhood-question. Of how stressful that had been for her poor broody husband. Of how it meant she now had an obligation to Daniel to be *100%* behind whatever he wanted to try, to champion, when it came to improving their chances of conceiving. Even *if* those plans included highlighting how unfit she was, she winced, thinking back to the unexpected turn their "walk" in the countryside had taken yesterday...

Her cheeks flushed all over again as she recalled the breathless, sweaty mess their unforeseen, uphill jog had turned her into. Honestly, it had been quite embarrassing to stand in front of her husband after that exertion, panting like a wild dog.

Daniel hadn't *meant* to make her feel small by putting her through her paces like that, though. Had he? She was hit with a teeny moment of doubt, before shaking her head. No, of course not. That was a ridiculous thought. He was her *husband*! He'd never deliberately put her down! Right? All he'd been trying to do was prove there *were* still areas where she could improve her health, i.e. in her cardiovascular fitness. An improvement that might make the difference between a baby happening or not. Of course, plenty of sedentary, overweight people effortlessly fell pregnant every day ... but since she wasn't one of those lucky people she, just like Daniel said, had to try harder to make her body baby-ready.

With that thought in mind, she quickly replied to his text with an upbeat smiley face *and* a thumbs-up emoji, to show just how on board she was with whatever he wanted from her. Before she sent it she added a couple of kisses, because she noted *he* hadn't included even one of those on his message. Which was pretty unusual for Daniel, actually. Unless he was in a rush or a grumpy mood he always signed off his texts to her with a kiss – or three!

It probably didn't mean anything, she tried to tell herself.

And yet...

And yet, it made Lacey think of something else from yesterday – the moment his mum had asked if he had anything nice planned for their wedding anniversary this month. It was a day *she* was looking forward to celebrating because, for her, their wedding had been a moment of utter joy. She'd almost danced down the aisle that crisp December morning, so ecstatic had she felt at becoming Daniel's wife! And she was already prepared with a gorgeous embossed card and a personalised gift to give him to mark the milestone: seeing as cotton was the theme for a two-year anniversary, she'd ordered a pair of his 'n hers Egyptian cotton towels, embroidered with their names and a love heart. Which might sound a funny present for a bloke, but Daniel *loved* anything home-interiors-related!

Or, at least, she frowned, she hoped he'd love her gift. Because nothing about him seemed quite the same as it used to, right now. And that included the way he'd reacted to his mum's question about their upcoming anniversary – he'd practically *grimaced* at the topic being raised, Lacey recalled nervously. Which was quite a contrast to last year, when he'd made a lovely fuss around their first wedding anniversary. Fuss that had involved writing her the sweetest, mushiest love letter (one year was represented by paper, after all!); followed by champagne, heart-shaped chocolates and what-felt-like endless kisses under the covers for an entire weekend...

Her heart panged at the memory.

Truly, this year, she didn't care whether Daniel wanted to organise something nice for them both, as a way of celebrating the day; or even whether he had a gift or a card for her in return.

All she really wanted was, even just for a second or two, for him to look at her the way he used to. For him to shoot her an easy grin, pull her into his arms, murmur something soppy in her ear. Give her a sign, just one little sign, that he ... he *was* still happy to be married to her. That his grimace of yesterday, even his easily-flustered mood of late, didn't mean what, deep down, she was worried it might.

Namely, that he regretted being tied to a marriage that wasn't giving him what he wanted. What he needed: a family of his own.

Once she got started with her group therapy session, however, there was no room in Lacey's mind to keep worrying about her husband. Not when one glance around the circle of participants showed a sea of anxious faces looking back at her. Anxiousness that, as each client began to open up about what was concerning them, sure enough turned out to be tied in one way or another to the festive season. How to deal with the shouty-supermarket-promotions on bumper sized boxes of chocolates and biscuits? one girl, Mary, asked, looking near to tears as she recounted how difficult she found food shopping in December. The scrutiny that would come on Christmas Day itself, when he'd be expected to sit down and eat with extended family members, was troubling another, a young lad called Ricky.

Lacey's heart wobbled as she listened attentively to her group's concerns. She wished she could just sprinkle some sort of Christmas glitter around the room, that would magically allow each and every one of her patients to be free of their woes, at least for the holiday period! Wished she could gift them all a happy, carefree, joyful Christmas, just like the ones you saw in dreamy movies set in a snowy New York or a lit-up, bustling London. They were all working so hard on their recoveries, it was the least they deserved.

As it was, she only had her training – and her helpful handbook – to offer them. But she made sure, through the hour, to give each person as much advice as she could (*"Practice lots of self-care; Use your grounding techniques; Don't forget you're never alone with this – you can call the clinic anytime,* **and** *there's a national helpline over Christmas"*). By the end of the workshop she was rewarded by a definite easing in the angst on her clients' faces, which helped her own heart feel a little less burdened, too.

By the time everyone had left and she'd tidied the room of used coffee cups, Lacey realised she was due to go on lunch break. So, on the way back to her office, she made a stop at the staff kitchen to fix herself a mint tea and pick up her Tupperware box from the fridge. She was starving, she realised, peeling back the lid to see what was inside. Hoping, as she did so, for something filling! (She didn't know what she might find, you see ... because Daniel had long since taken over prepping her midday meals.)

Before she could take a peek, though, she was interrupted by her phone vibrating in her pocket. Another message from Daniel, she realised:

Enjoy your carrot sticks and hummus. Lots of protein and Vitamin A – so good for you! P.S. Don't worry, it's homemade hummus – no oil involved!!

Oh. Lacey eyed her Tupperware container in disappointment. *That's* what was inside? Carrot sticks and, er, olive-oil-free hummus?! Right. *Right*. As the kettle boiled, her gaze drifted to the window and she tried not to shiver as she noticed the weather: it was pelting down with rain outside, and the wind was battering the glass, into the bargain. She couldn't deny carrot sticks 'n hummus would probably be quite a refreshing combination on a hot summer's day. But, today? Oh. Today, a big steaming bowl of soup with a hunk of bread and butter would've been much more welcome, she thought longingly.

She realised she was practically drooling at the thought of that bread and butter (butter had been banned from their own fridge for months now, because dairy *might* negatively impact fertility – something to do with inflammation – Daniel had declared, one day back in early summer). But then she checked herself. Because she knew, if her husband could read her mind right now, he'd probably start hopping around like a highly-strung hare, nervous to see her having cravings for naughty foods (or, at least, foods that were naughty in *his* eyes). Besides, she should be grateful he'd gone to the effort of making her lunch at all – especially something healthy *and* homemade! How many husbands would do that on a regular basis?!

On that note, she sent him a thank you message, then grabbed her tea and Tupperware box and headed back to her office. She shared the room with her fellow psychology assistant, Cooper, who she really enjoyed working alongside, given his easy-going nature. He always looked pretty cool into the bargain, with his shaved-sides afro, smattering of dark stubble, and wardrobe full of Nike sweatpants and t-shirts.

It turned out, though, that Cooper wasn't the only person hanging out in their office this lunchtime... because, when she walked through the door, the first thing Lacey saw was his girlfriend, Charlotte, perched on the edge of his desk.

She smiled to herself as she watched her friend giggle and toss her long ringlets. Because Charlotte wasn't just Cooper's other half – she was also Lacey's mate and colleague. In fact, *they* used to share this office together, back when they'd both been psychology assistants, fresh out of university. But then Charlotte had gone and nabbed herself a promotion – and an office of her very own, just along the hall – thanks to the fact she'd completed a further master's degree in Clinical Psychology last year.

'Hey honey! Good to see you. How's your day going?' Charlotte turned to give her a little wave, showing off vivid red nails.

'Great, thanks,' Lacey sat down and opened her lunchbox. 'I'm just on break now.'

'Good. We won't disturb you working, then,' Charlotte declared. She pointed at Cooper's computer screen, where Lacey realised a YouTube video was playing. 'I was just showing Boston Common to Cooper, see. You can't wait to visit, can you?!'

Cooper grinned up at his girlfriend. As he did, you couldn't miss how starry-eyed he looked. Aw – how cute! Lacey's insides melted a little at the sight. He and Charlotte – they'd only been dating for just over a year (they, just like her mother-in-law and Neville, had also got together at the Grace Hall Halloween party last October. Which, given the pairings it seemed to have acted as a catalyst for, Lacey mused, was really quite strange – because the party had *definitely* been rocking a spooky, rather than syrupy, vibe!).

Anyway. The two seemed really happy together. So happy, they were jetting off to Boston, Massachusetts for Christmas this year, which was where Charlotte originally hailed from.

'I really can't,' he agreed. 'I can't wait to meet your mum and dad, too.'

'They're gonna love you, sweetie,' Charlotte simpered. Then she turned back to Lacey and tittered. 'Oh sorry, honey. We must be making you *super*-jealous! Shame you and Daniel can't join us, because Boston is *the* most awesome place to spend the holidays. We're gonna go ice skating at Frog Pond and stuff our faces with my mom's incredible pecan pie...'

Pecan pie? *Oh my*. Lacey paused, mid-crunch, on a carrot stick, and felt a jolt of longing. She'd never tried the sweet delicacy, but it certainly sounded delicious!

'...and I'm gonna show Cooper off to all my girlfriends, too, obviously,' Charlotte continued. She winked at her boyfriend, before adding. 'I mean, everyone back home thinks it's, like, awesome I live in England, and that I've got an Englishman on my arm! But I wanna make sure they really know how well I'm doing. So I've bought a new, chic winter wardrobe to wear while I'm there ... actually, I'm wearing some of it already!' She giggled as she waved at her figure-hugging jumper dress and black knee-high boots.

'Plus I'm booked in to have my hair done before we fly. And I've got a second suitcase full of British-themed pressies to treat everyone with, too. Like Yorkshire fruit cake and English Rose soaps. Oh, Cooper.' She clapped her hands together in delight. 'I really, *really* can't wait for us to get on the plane!!'

Cooper laughed indulgently, before reaching out and squeezing his girlfriend's knee. And Lacey – well, Charlotte's excitement was so infectious, she felt an unexpected flash of joy, too! It was nice, after the anxiousness around the holiday season she'd felt in her group therapy session, to see the flip side of the coin. To see someone *soo* looking forward to Christmas. To hear plans that really did sound like they were out of an idyllic festive movie!

Plus, Charlotte more than deserved this happiness, Lacey knew, because last year she'd gone through a bit of a rough time. Before Cooper had come on the scene, she'd actually been married, to Daniel's best mate Rob. Unfortunately it was a marriage that had lasted barely five minutes; and its unravelling had left her friend with a crisis of confidence, especially when it came to trusting the opposite sex again. But since being brave enough to admit to the feelings she'd begun having for Cooper, Charlotte seemed to have gone from strength to strength in rebuilding her life. It was really good to see her back to her old sassy, shiny self ... just in time for Christmas! Lacey smiled.

As she watched the pair laugh and entwine hands, though, Lacey also couldn't help but feel a flash of regret: they looked so infatuated, and it reminded her of how she and Daniel had been – *last* December! Following her announcement last year that she was finally ready to get on board with her husband's dream of having a baby, you see, their relationship had blossomed all over again. Which had been idyllic! Lacey recalled. It also meant, last Christmas, they'd spent most of the holiday period gazing dreamily at one another over gingerbread lattes or taking romantic walks in the snow, where they'd held hands and giggled about how amazing it felt to be starting a new chapter of their lives. They'd talked, endlessly, of how exciting the next year was going to be, once the new member of their family arrived. Had told each other, over and over again, *I love you* and *You're going to be the BEST parent ever!*, the way couples planning a child always did.

How naïve they'd been! Lacey swallowed. To think the future they craved was just going to fall into their laps.

How naïve indeed...

Her reminiscing was interrupted by her phone pinging with yet another message from Daniel:

Just a reminder, babe – make sure you drink loads of water today. You need to keep hydrated to have healthy cervical mucus!

Healthy cervical mucus?! Well, that was certainly a phrase she'd never expected to hear drop from her husband's lips, Lacey lamented.

She looked back at Charlotte and Cooper, who were now smiling together as they watched a magical-looking video of ice skaters twirling on the frozen Frog Pond in Boston, under a canopy of fairy lights strung across nearby trees. Then she bit back a sigh, pushed her phone away ... and returned to resolutely sticking hunks of carrot into her lumpy little pot of homemade hummus.

*

Later, when her working day was over, Lacey didn't head home like usual – because she had plans for her evening which involved staying in the centre of York. She was heading to the F-Group meet-up her grandma had mentioned, when they'd bumped into one another at the market on Saturday.

The drive from The Serenity Clinic to the place they were congregating – the library on Museum Street – was a slow one, given the rush hour traffic. But Lacey found she didn't mind. She had the city's Christmas lights, vibrant against the dark December sky, to admire as she crawled along the road. She was also quite happy, if she was honest, to be heading *away* from the direction of home ... because it meant some extra time away from her husband. Which might sound mean, but she just needed a little break from the incessant requests – "*Drink more water*"; "*Don't work too hard*"; and, a new one: "*Don't forget to eat the roasted chickpeas I packed in your bag for an afternoon snack*" – he'd been throwing her way all day long. (Although admittedly, her phone had ceased pinging *quite* so much through the afternoon. Probably because, by that point, Daniel had headed out to do a little Christmas shopping of his own, at the designer outlet on the outskirts of the city).

More than anything, though, she was excited about *why* the F-Group were getting together tonight...

When she finally arrived at her destination, Lacey knew there'd been a change to the room the group usually used as the location for their meetings. There was a very good reason for that, she smiled, as she headed up the library staircase and entered an unfamiliar, high-ceilinged space – typically hired out as a venue for conferences – that was nearly three times as large as their usual meeting place.

One glance at a stack of leaflets on a nearby chair told the whole story. Leaflets she herself had handed out at work, and to neighbours and friends, over the past few weeks:

This December, F-Group are hosting a very special CHRISTMAS PARTY!

Join us, for a magical night of mistletoe, mince pies and mulled wine.

Tickets available online – get yours NOW!

Yup. That was right. This year, the F-Group had decided to hold a Christmas Party – in this very room! But not just because they wanted an excuse to get-merry-on-sherry and dance to Brenda Lee's "Rockin' Around the Christmas Tree". The event was actually a fundraiser.

A fundraiser for a *very* good cause.

A cause that Lacey felt, sadly, more connected to, than she would've liked...

'Lacey! Great, you're here. Take this, will you. I've loads more boxes in the car I need to unpack.'

Hearing her mum's voice, Lacey turned, to see Sadie in the doorway behind her. She was peering over the top of a *mammoth* cardboard box, one which she was trying to manoeuvre into the room. Thrillingly, it looked to be full of Christmas decorations, given the stray reams of tinsel trailing out of the top.

Lacey was instantly reminded that those decorations were the whole reason behind tonight's get-together. Given that the F-Group party was happening just a few days from now, on Saturday night, it was time to make a start on transforming this boring, white-walled conference room into a sparkly party space!

She hurried over to take the box from her mum's arms ... but nearly collapsed to the floor under the unexpected weight of the thing. 'Oof. This is heavy.'

'Is it?' her mum frowned. 'I didn't realise.'

Sometimes, Lacey thought wryly, as she struggled towards a nearby table where she could dump the box, she forgot how strong her mum was. And it was all thanks to the many hours she spent whacking a punch bag at her boyfriend Maz's gym every week!

Not that Sadie had taken up kickboxing as a hobby, like most people did, Lacey had to acknowledge.

No. She … she'd taken it up, so she could learn to fight. Or, at least, that's what had driven her interest in the sport, right back at the beginning.

That thought made Lacey pause in opening the box of decorations. Instead, she glanced around her. Realised other F-Group volunteers were beginning to arrive to help out, too. There was a real mix to the group: local university students – female *and* male – with nose piercings and slouchy jeans; a group of older ladies who, no matter the weather, always seemed to be clad in zip-up fleeces; a Scottish husband 'n wife – Eleanor and Tam – who loved to bring a box of homemade shortbread along to each and every meeting!

One by one they shrugged off their winter coats. Called out greetings to each other. Exclaimed over how well ticket sales had gone (they'd completely sold out!). Lacey could tell, from their smiling faces, how eager they were to get stuck in to the task of the night. To get started in hanging giant-sized, shiny baubles from the ceiling and decorate tables with Christmas crackers and snowflake-shaped confetti, all with the purpose of creating a festive backdrop for Saturday night.

She tried to feel her way back in to their happy vibe. But it was difficult when her thoughts had just slid backwards. Back to the reason her mum had wanted to learn how to defend herself, through kickboxing. Back to the reason, too, why *she'd* been so motivated to support the F-Group's Christmas event this year…

She swallowed, thinking of how the whole purpose behind the party the F-Group were hosting was to raise funds for a very particular and important cause: namely, to support a local women's refuge known as "The Cocoon". The charity had had their government funding cut a while back, and was struggling to stay afloat as a result. Her mum actually worked at the centre – had done, for years – as a Domestic Abuse Support Worker. So she'd been able to pass on to the group first-hand knowledge of how vital the service was, in giving women – and more often than not their children, too – a safe escape route from the unhappy circumstance of a home-life-turned-bad, thanks to an abusive partner.

But her mum's personal involvement at The Cocoon, in the bewildered and broken victims that found themselves there, wasn't the only reason everyone wanted this fundraiser to be a success…

Lacey felt a flutter of sorrow as she considered how both her and her mum's lives had been *personally tainted* by domestic abuse. Not that she remembered anything about the awful situation – she'd only been a baby in her mum's tummy when it had been going on. She only knew what had happened ... because of the enduring absence of a dad in her life.

A dad her mum had had to escape, before she was even born, because of the violence he'd embraced. Because of his ... his raging temper and thumping-Sadie-to-a-bruised-pulp ways. Her heart twisted painfully, as it always did, at the thought of what her mum had had to endure, all those years ago.

Sadie had relied on a domestic violence charity to help *her* get away from her vicious partner. After that, she'd made it her life's work to help other women who inadvertently found themselves in the same situation. (Of course, men were victims of domestic abuse, too, Lacey acknowledged, and were just as deserving of help. But she also knew the grim, statistically-proven reality: *substantially more* females endured *sustained* emotional, physical and sexual violence than men, every single year. It was a fact that never failed to upset her.)

At least, she quickly told herself, with another glance around the bustling room, everyone here (plus everyone who'd bought a ticket to the party or donated decorations or a prize for the raffle they'd hold on the night) was doing something to try and change that desperate situation. That was true Christmas spirit, wasn't it? she nodded. To give your time, energy, charity, to helping the less fortunate?

That thought helped restore Lacey's mood to a brighter place. And then she noticed her mum had returned to the room – this time she was, determinedly and single-handedly, lugging a towering Christmas tree through the doorway!

'Sheila brought this in the van,' Sadie explained, as Lacey ran over to help her. Not that she seemed to need assistance: there wasn't even one drop of sweat on her forehead from dragging the tree all the way up the stairs!

'It's gorgeous,' Lacey enthused, imagining how pretty it was going to look, decorated and lit up as a centrepiece to the party. 'It's so tall we're going to need stepladders to dress it– oh.'

She broke off as a funny feeling unexpectedly stole over her. A feeling of ... well, of wooziness, so bad she had to grab at a nearby chair for support.

As her head spun, Lacey realised she'd felt this exact same sensation yesterday, too. It'd come over her after Daniel had urged her to jog up that frosty field, hadn't it? In fact, when she'd come to a stop, at the top of the incline, she'd been so dizzy she'd had to clutch at his arm for fear she might faint clean away!

Oh, dear. She frowned, hoping she wasn't coming down with a winter bug.

'Lacey? Lacey, are you OK? Sheila, here, take this.'

Sadie thrust the Christmas tree at her friend, then grabbed Lacey's arm and told her to sit down.

'Are you OK? What's going on?'

Lacey explained she'd just had a funny turn. That, like yesterday, she was sure she'd be fine in a minute or two.

Her mum barked out an order for someone to fetch a glass of water.

'Here, drink this. And take a few deep breaths.'

Lacey did as she was told, and soon began to feel better. In truth, though, she wasn't sure if that was down to resting for a moment or ... or whether it was actually because of the way her mum was gentle stroking her hair as she breathed in and out.

The sensation was so nice, her whole body began to relax. Then she glanced up and saw concern all over Sadie's face, concern that made her heart tremble.

Oh! Although feeling dizzy wasn't nice ... it was almost worth feeling a little out-of-sorts, if it meant getting fussed over by her mum. Which probably sounded an odd thing to say; but Sadie's softer side wasn't something that'd featured much in her life. In years gone by, even if she'd been puking into the toilet bowl courtesy of a bout of food poisoning, her mum wouldn't have had any sympathy. Would have simply scowled and snapped at her to "Woman up!" and stop being "so soft".

Lacey had come to understand why Sadie had been that way, though. It all went back to the domestic abuse she'd suffered. That violence – it had hardened her. Made her steely, cold. She'd put massive barriers in place between herself and anyone who might hurt her, and had been determined to raise her daughter to be just as fierce. Thankfully, last year Sadie had begun to see that sneering and scowling her way through life wasn't really a great strategy for protecting *anybody*, including herself. That all it did, in fact, was push her loved ones away.

To that end – and to Lacey *and* Sadie's partner, Maz's, relief – she'd finally come to accept that she needed help in dealing with the trauma she'd gone through...

One year, and multiple therapy sessions later, and Lacey honestly felt she could burst with pride at the changes her mum had embraced! She'd started to let her guard down a little in life. Had begun to love a little easier, too. Which wasn't just wonderful to see. It was wonderful to *feel*, Lacey nodded, as her mum continued to sweetly stroke her hair, making her feel almost like a cherished, happy little kid!

Not, of course, that Sadie's healing journey had turned her completely marshmallow-esque or anything like that! Her mum could never lose her inner warrior. Especially when it came to fighting for her sisters. In fact – Lacey couldn't help but smile as her eyes dropped to the words printed on Sadie's sweatshirt: *Destroy the patriarchy, not the planet!* it determinedly declared.

Eventually, her dizzy spelled passed. After that, her mum let her return to helping the rest of the group unpack box after box of sparkly decorations. The atmosphere in the room became so chatty and fun and festive, she soon forgot about her funny turn and, instead, laughed and strung fairy lights and paper-chains along with everybody else. Then, at some point in the evening, her grandma turned up. Supposedly to help set out napkins, bamboo cutlery and paper cups on the buffet table; but Lacey couldn't help but notice, wryly, that every time she glanced round she found Rose sitting in a chair, seemingly perfectly content to just *watch* what was going on ... whilst simultaneously scoffing chunk after chunk of shortbread from the fresh batch Eleanor and Tam had brought along tonight!

She also noticed that, at one point, Sheila went over and asked if Rose would like to help dress the tree. Her grandma replied, "Thank you, but no", in such a firm tone, that Sheila frowned. Until, that was, Rose sniggered and declared she'd "already done more than enough to help out with organising the party"; and that Sheila would "understand what she meant" on Saturday night. It was a slightly-mysterious remark that, for a brief moment, had Lacey thinking again of the equally-mystifying black bin liner her grandma had been lugging around the Christmas market at the weekend...

Time ticked on. They were so busy, it was only when they all stopped for a well-deserved tea break (which, for Lacey, involved brewing her own fruit tea, given caffeine was also on her Forbidden List right now) that she realised she'd received another new message from Daniel at some point during the evening. Given she'd left her bag at the side of the room, she hadn't heard her phone ping.

Please don't be late home, he'd written. *It's nice you're helping your mum tonight, but don't overdo it. You need a fresh body if you want to have healthy hormones! See you soon, hey?*

Er. Right. Fair point, Lacey supposed ... even if the latter part of his message sounded like something an over-enthusiastic fertility coach might spout (and yes, there *was* such a thing as a "fertility coach" – people who supported and encouraged your journey to conceiving a child; Daniel had stumbled upon the concept one day, when he'd been Googling "Tips to get pregnant FAST").

When she glanced at the time the message had been sent, though, Lacey felt a jolt of alarm – because it was only then that she saw it had been delivered to her phone over an hour ago.

She winced, hoping Daniel wouldn't think she'd been ignoring him. Or, worse, disregarding what he wanted of her, seeing as she was still out and about, instead of back home already (*See you soon, hey?*). Which might sound overly-paranoid, or even overly-obedient, of her. But ... well.

Once upon a time, she sighed, her husband couldn't have cared less what time she came home from *anything*! And she meant that in a nice, laid-back, kind-of-a-way. He'd never been a controlling guy. Ever.

But, lately... She thought of his anxious face when she hadn't jumped up to immediately do her yoga moves on Saturday night. Of the panic and ... and irritation in his voice, when he'd seen for himself how unfit she was, after her hopeless attempt at jogging yesterday. Of the relentless instructions he'd been sending her way all day long.

Daniel was different than he used to be. That much was obvious. But she couldn't blame him for that! These were *different times*, after all. They had worries on their shoulders that never used to be there. Awful worries, about if and how they were *ever* going to fall pregnant.

And those worries, she reminded herself, might have been non-existent if they'd started trying for a baby earlier, using the precious time she'd instead wasted, dithering over whether having a child was something that could actually be possible for her.

That last thought was enough to remind Lacey she was doing the right thing, in being agreeable to everything her husband wanted, when it came to making her body a ... a perfect temple for reproducing or whatever. It was the only way to prove to him how sorry she was, for the reluctance she'd subjected him to last year around the idea of their starting a family. The only way to prove to him how completely committed she was, *nowadays*, to the idea of a baby.

On that note ... Lacey glanced around. The conference room was beginning to look much chirpier and cheerier, thanks to everyone at F-Group's hard work and the umpteen garlands, gold stars and glass baubles they'd draped and dressed the place with over the last few hours. But there were still jobs to be done: more stray boxes to unpack; chairs to set out; plus she knew, too, that Sadie and Sheila wanted to go over the catering and cloakroom plans for Saturday night.

She bit her lip, realising she was going to have to bail on all of that. It didn't matter, though – she loved Daniel so much, she'd do nearly anything for him.

She grabbed her jacket and hurried over to say goodbye to her mum and grandma.

SEVEN

Tuesday morning found Daniel back at the gift shop, unboxing new orders of sparkly necklaces and gemstone earrings that he hoped tourists to the hall would quickly snap up as Christmas gifts. He was finding it really quite a satisfying job, to rip open the outer cardboard containers. Probably because he could throw his weight behind the task, could use it as a way – courtesy of yanking and tearing at the thick packaging tape – of working out a little of the jittery vibe he was filled with today.

That was how he'd woken up that morning, you see – feeling as keyed-up as an impatient Black Friday shopper, two minutes before mall opening time...

Not that he wanted to feel that way. It wasn't particularly pleasant to have his tummy wrapping itself into tight knots. It seemed, though, like he had no choice in the matter. Try as he might – he'd even sipped a camomile tea for breakfast! – he couldn't seem to get his mind to stop fizzing towards edginess.

He thought back to yesterday, to the events he knew had triggered his tense state today.

First of all, he'd gone Christmas shopping. Which should've been a fun thing to do, right? Especially since he'd headed out to a cool designer outlet on the outskirts of the city. He'd thought it would be a nice place to find a few gifts for Lacey, and his mum. Maybe, he'd mused, he'd even find something for Neville – some aftershave, or a pair of new slippers. He'd been looking forward, too, to a smoothie stop mid-way through the afternoon, at one of the numerous nice cafés dotted throughout the centre.

And he *had* done those things. And, mostly, he'd enjoyed his day out. But if he was honest, while he'd been at the outlet, he'd also felt quite out of place. The reason being, everywhere he'd flipping looked, he'd been faced with the ever-so-sweet sight of mums and dads out shopping with their babies and toddlers in tow! On every corner, it had seemed, there'd been chubby-cheeked cherubs, giggling in their prams; or pattering around on wobbly legs, to peer curiously at shop windows full of ribbon-wrapped gift boxes and flashing Christmas lights.

Although he had, of course, smiled at the cuteness of the kids around him, the sight had also made a tight lump grow in his throat. Jealousy, too, had seeped into him. The worst jealousy he'd ever felt, actually, when it came to other people having the gorgeous children that he simply didn't. He wasn't sure why. Maybe it was something to do with how much kids were tied up with the fun of the Christmas season. Or maybe it was simply because, month on month of bad news on the pregnancy-test-front was growing his worry and agitation as to whether he'd *ever* be a dad, to increasingly torturous proportions. Whatever the reason – and however horrible and bitter it sounded for him to admit to such a feeling – the hot, resentful, why-wasn't-*he*-one-of-those-dads envy that had filled his bones, had been so strong he was still loaded down with it today.

Maybe, in hindsight, he shouldn't have chosen the outlet for his shopping trip. He supposed he could understand why he'd been surrounded by so many family groups there. He glanced outside, to where rain was thudding down on Grace Hall's gardens. The wind was howling, too, so badly the building's old window frames were rattling and groaning under the strain. Given the weather had been this stormy for the last few days, was it really any wonder parents with prams would congregate at somewhere like the designer outlet, where all the shops were housed in a cosy, covered mall? It had to be better than traipsing their way around a damp, exposed York centre, where they'd have to struggle with PVC rain covers and waterproof macs as they dived in and out of each separate store!

Anyway. As the rain continued to beat against the windows Daniel also noticed it was awfully dark outside. It really was a proper, bleak winter's day, and he wondered if that was why the shop had been quiet all morning – who'd be enticed to tour a stately home in these gloomy conditions, when the gardens would most likely be off-limits, too? (Unless you wanted to get drenched and blown around like a brittle autumn leaf caught in a swirl of wind, that was!)

He found he didn't really mind if he didn't have many customers today. He wasn't particularly in the mood for small talk, for pretending to be in a cheery, *Christmas-is-coming!* mood, when that was so at odds with how he really felt.

Still. Daniel had to admit it wasn't just yesterday's shopping trip that'd triggered today's angst...

An image of his wife, nervously appearing through the front door of their cottage last night – *late* last night – flashed into his mind. It made him chew frantically on the inside of his cheek.

Thing was, yesterday, Lacey had gone straight from work, to help her mum set up for the F-Group Christmas party. Which had been fine. Nice of her, actually. Given the very good cause the event was fundraising for, he was proud of his wife's efforts.

What he hadn't expected, was how late she'd end up staying out! Not to sound like a dictator-esque husband, but he preferred her to retreat to bed earlier these days – sleep was good for your health and, given she'd be ovulating soon, it was *super* important she got maximum rest, to make sure nothing interfered with that process.

She definitely hadn't looked rested when she'd finally come home, he recalled. She'd looked pale, tired, nervous, even, for some reason.

But over-doing things and getting stressed, tired – worse, both! – was only going to hamper their conception plans. It really was. At this point he'd read *so much* about how being fresh-in-body and calm-in-mind could help the body feel it was in a safe state to fall pregnant. Of course, people could – and did –

conceive in flipping war zones so, Daniel scratched his head, he wasn't sure that theory was *entirely* correct... Still, as a couple, they weren't in a position to argue against *any* fertility advice right now, were they?

Which made it even more frustrating, he nodded, to think of how Lacey had willingly put decorating a party venue above her own health yesterday. And the proof he wasn't over-reacting, that she *had* done exactly that, was in the way she'd stumbled home last night, looking drawn and exhausted!

Oh. He shook his head, feeling almost drained with worry. Worry that'd been on his shoulders for far too long now. Why was life throwing them this horrible problem in the first place? Why couldn't they be like Ella and Olly, who he knew for a fact were excitedly stocking up on toys and treats to prepare for "Santa's" first-ever visit to Lina on the 25th December? Or gleefully visiting Santa's Grotto, just like Rob and Abby had done at the weekend with Milo?

It just wasn't fair. But of course, he also knew they were far from the only people in this *want-a-baby-but-it-just-isn't-happening* position. He read plenty of sorrowful posts on infertility forums these days to know that. Really, there was a *sea* of sadness out there, when it came to couples not being able to conceive their own child. People didn't talk about it enough in everyday life, that was for sure.

He sighed aloud then, after double-checking the contents of his jewellery order against the invoice, headed down to the far end of the shop. There, where the store's large, mirrored jewellery cabinets were housed, he decided to try and switch his focus to the task of putting his new stock out on display. Because all these relentless, difficult thoughts were doing nothing except make his head throb!

Just as he was determinedly fixing sparkly earrings to silver display stands, though, something happened – on the ceiling high above him, the spotlights suddenly flickered. On and off, on and off, they went, before settling down again.

Daniel looked up with a frown. Hm. He'd never known *that* to happen before. Maybe, he surmised, the flickering had been caused by an electrical surge? To do with the stormy weather outside?

He shrugged, then returned to unboxing sets of pretty pearl earrings. But then another strange thing happened.

Icy air swept across the back of his neck. And he meant, *seriously* icy air. Like an Arctic blast or something! Despite the fact the cast iron radiators in the shop were all propelling out hot air, he shivered, as violently as though he'd got caught in a snow storm wearing only his fine mesh running vest!

How odd.

He glanced round, wondering if one of the windows had been blown open by the wind. How else to explain such a gust of freezing air driving its way through the previously-comfortable room?

But all the sashes, though rattling in the howling wind, appeared firmly shut.

A beat later, and the cool air seemed to disperse. Daniel began to warm up again. The lights remained steady, too. He shot one last, searching glance around the store, then shrugged again.

Maybe, somehow, given the wind was so strong today, a flurry of cold air had worked its way through from the rear door of the hall? Unlikely, yes; but not impossible, surely? Especially given that imposing stately homes like this one weren't exactly known for having the kind of snug 'n cosy vibe a little cottage might!

He returned to unpacking the new freshwater pearl jewellery, pausing to peer at an eye-catching silver 'n pearl necklace he thought might make a nice stocking filler for his mum. Especially since he got a staff discount on anything he bought from Grace Hall! Yes, he'd set one of those aside to add to his own Christmas shopping haul, he decided–

Just at that, he was disturbed once more. This time, though, it was by the sound of footsteps.

Heavy, thudding footsteps, which he'd noticed start up in the corridor outside the store a few moments ago – but which, strangely, didn't seem to be settling down, or drifting away.

Instead, up and down, up and down, they went, as though someone was pacing the old oak floor.

That's odd, he thought. Because, when they reached this point of the tour, most visitors to the house would at least pop their heads into the gift shop...

'D ...aaa... nieeel.'

What the–?

Above the sound of the footsteps he suddenly heard something else. A murmur, that echoed around the lofty room. It sounded awfully like somebody was saying his name; only the sound was distorted, as though they were calling out from the other end of a long tunnel.

Daniel swallowed, set down the pearl necklace and, this time, turned to face the store head-on. But the place was still empty, with not a customer in sight. There was nobody behind him that could be muttering *anything*, never mind his name.

He quickly decided to blame the noise on the gales outside, too. He'd simply mistaken the sounds of the blustery day for an actual, er, word. Right?!

He knew he couldn't blame the wind for the footsteps that were still thudding on outside the shop door, though. And he ... he couldn't blame it for the funny, woozy feeling that abruptly came over him, either.

Oh. He blinked, as the room suddenly spun around in front of his eyes. He pressed a hand to his forehead, trying to collect himself.

A beat later, and the feeling passed.

But the becoming-annoying-now footsteps *still* didn't let up.

Daniel began to feel a bit uneasy. The dark, stormy day. The flickering lights. The gust of icy air. The relentless footfall, belonging to someone who wasn't showing their face...

He was probably being paranoid. None of that was anything to be rattled by. Was it?

And yet–

And yet, try as he might to settle his flip-flopping heart, Daniel couldn't help the way his mind whipped back, once again, to the unsettling happenings that had been quite the feature of his time at Grace Hall.

Slowly, warily, he found himself being drawn towards the shop door. He simply couldn't help it. He had to know who – or what – was lurking out there. So he took a deep breath, braced himself ... then peered ever-so-anxiously into the hallway beyond.

'*Alreet*, lad. How's it going? By, it's a quiet day, isn't it? I've been wandering from room to room, trying to find some visitors to offer a "Happy Holidays" greeting to. But no such luck!'

Oh. *Stevie?!* Aka St Nicholas? *He* was the person behind the unabating footsteps?! Daniel blushed as his eyes met those of Lady Tuncaster's hired-historical-Santa-Claus. And then he pressed a hand to his chest, relieved to find it was simply his imagination running wild that'd once again gotten him all spooked out!

Not that he, *ahem*, wanted to let on to a guy as big and stout as Stevie that he'd got all worked up by his unexpected presence outside the store. (The guy usually hung around the entrance foyer, you see.) So he stuffed his trembling hands into his pockets and quickly agreed it *was* a quiet day. 'It might pick up after lunch,' he added.

'Let's hope so,' Stevie nodded. Then he shot Daniel a wave before wandering off in his swishy, bishop-esque cloak, peering into room after room as he made his way down the long corridor.

Daniel, watching him go, wryly shook his head. Honestly. Yes, it was perfectly understandable – after the ghostly run-ins he'd experienced these past couple of years – that unexplained noises and footsteps (and fellows-in-olde-worlde-costumes!) would make him uneasy, in a way people who *hadn't* bumped into the, er, walking, talking dead probably couldn't quite understand. But it had been months and months since his last spooky encounter at Grace Hall. Which meant the chances of meeting any more spirits around the place now surely stood at zero. Right?!

Right, Daniel nodded determinedly. So he had to get a grip on this nervousness of his, he decided. Be a little steadier. Braver, even. On that note he turned and headed, with purpose, back into the gift shop ... only to let out the most enormous shriek a mere two seconds later.

What the–?

He came to a juddering halt. Like a cartoon character, he felt his eyes nearly pop out of his head at the sight he was unexpectedly met with.

OK. The shop had *definitely* been empty of any other person when he'd left it, mere moments ago.

But now – his jaw dropped – there was a man standing in front of him.

Not just any man, though...

EIGHT

The seconds ticked past. Rain lashed on against the windows. And, Daniel – he continued to gawp.

Gawp, at the man before him.

A man, who was dressed in a smart dark suit, upturned white collar and shiny black shoes. A man who had a ... a top hat on his head. A top hat he reached up and tipped in Daniel's direction.

'Ah, there you are, boy! Good morning! Didn't you hear me calling you? I thought you'd clean run out on me,' he declared, in a crisp, hoity-toity voice.

It was a voice Daniel knew well. In fact, it was as familiar to him as the new arrival's face...

His heart pounded in shock.

Wh ... what the heck was going on?

Wilfred?!

Except, it couldn't be, he gulped. This bloke ... he might, for some reason, look – and sound – exactly like his old friend.

Exactly like him.

But it couldn't actually *be* him. Right?!

He gulped again. Thought of how it had to be impossible. Literally *impossible*. That *Wilfred* – aka the long-dead 4th Earl of Tuncaster, and the very same man featured in the portrait he'd been looking at, at the top of the Grace Hall staircase last week – could once again be standing in front of him.

And yet–

He rubbed at his eyes. Blinked. Wondered if he was dreaming. But the more he gawped, the more he realised the likeness remained remarkable. Even this bloke's self-assured smirk matched that of his old buddy's!

But Wilfred – if the guy was indeed his old friend and not some illusion of his imagination – didn't seem to share Daniel's flabbergasted state. Instead, the spook calmly returned his top hat to his head, then impatiently waved something at him. Something that was clasped in his free hand.

'Good to see you and all that business, boy. But before we talk further I must ask – what in the good Lord's name is *this*?'

It took Daniel a second to tear his astonished gaze away from the old spook and, instead, focus on the item being thrust in his face. When he did, he clocked immediately what Wilfred was holding: a novelty figurine he must have picked up from the *Christmas Decorations* shelves. Specifically, a grinning elf with stripy socks and an overly-large head set on a spring, so it could bob up and down in a cheery fashion.

'That? Er. Well, it's a ... a bobblehead,' he found himself blurting (which were definitely *not* the first words he'd expected to utter, should he ever be reunited with his aristocratic buddy).

'A *what*? A *wobblehead*, you say?' Wilfred frowned and peered more closely at the elf. 'Well, fair play to the fellow. As you know, I had my own share of, *ahem*, wobbleheads, back in the day. It's a very good sign you've enjoyed the pleasures of a fine brandy, what?!' he chortled.

Daniel blinked. 'Er, no. Not a *wobblehead*. A bobblehead!' he corrected. 'His head shakes around. It's meant to be funny ... actually, never mind.' He shook his *own* head, remembering the poor elf toy Wilfred was insinuating to be some sort of drunkard wasn't really the focus here, was it?!

It was the fact that, once again, a long-dead Earl of Grace Hall was conversing with him. A long-dead Earl who was definitely meant to be lording it up in the afterlife, rather than swanning around a stately home gift shop (even if the bloke did happen to have, er, *owned* said stately home in his lifetime...).

It had been odd enough, Daniel recalled ruefully, to have made the guy's acquaintance first time around, back when he'd been an established Grace-Hall-ghost. A lonely creature, who'd been stuck in the shadows long after his death, thanks to an unresolved issue in his soul tying him to the earth plane.

But – thanks to psychic abilities he hadn't even known he possessed – he'd seen Wilfred settle those issues, leaving him free to move on. Move on to the true afterlife, where he'd hoped his old friend would find peace, and be reunited with his beloved wife.

So how, Daniel wondered again, was it possible his old friend could be standing here? Right in front of him? Had he *really* returned from The Other Side? And if so – how? And – more importantly – *why*?!

He needed answers. The only problem was, addressing Wilfred's abrupt re-entry into his life was so confusing, all he seemed able to stutter was: 'You ... you're *here*? But ...wh ... what ... *how* ... that is ... I mean...?'

'Hah. I see you're eloquent as ever, boy!' Wilfred snickered. He looked around at his surroundings, then let out a long exhale. 'Still, I must admit, I'm a tad speechless myself. This, you see,' he waved a hand at the gift shop, 'used to be a dashed fine Morning Room. I picked out the elegant silk sofas and antique Anatolian wool rug myself. Splendid pieces, they were, splendid indeed.

'Now,' he wandered around the shelving units, peering and prodding at things as he went, 'I find it's open to commoners and filled with ... with *wobbleheads* and ... what's this now?' He paused to pick up a box from the confectionary display, before exclaiming: '*Reindeer droppings*?!'

Oh. Right. 'N ... no, they're actually chocolate buttons,' Daniel explained. 'It's a novelty gift.'

Wilfred raised one eyebrow, then dropped the box back on the shelf with a rather disapproving *Harrumph!*

Hm. Yes. He always had been a bit snooty, Daniel recalled wryly. In fact – encouraged by the familiar show of snobbery – he took a stumbling step towards the ghost and finally managed to mumble, 'Wilfred? Is this really happening? Is ... is it really you? Truly?' He rubbed his eyes again. 'I'm *not* dreaming?!'

His old friend paused. Shot a lopsided smile across the room, before nodding.

'Correct, boy. It's really me. Now, tell me – have you missed me, old chap?!'

For a moment Daniel found all he could do was press his hands to his face in amazement. Then he hurried closer, feeling really quite emotional as he peered closely at his former buddy, taking in the crinkles around his bright blue eyes, and the pop of sandy-coloured hair underneath his swanky top hat.

Truth was, he thought he'd never see his old friend again. He cast his mind back, to a dark night, over two years ago now, when he'd left the ghost at the Grace Hall graveyard. He'd known, that night, that his friend was about to end his time in the hazy realm he'd got stuck in after his death, and make his journey to the true afterlife. Had known that, when he did so, he'd never be able to see or connect with the spook again. It had been a poignant moment and, even now, Daniel felt himself grow tearful at the memory. By that point, you see, he'd become really quite fond of Wilfred – strange though it might sound, to admit to having a bond with a spirit! But the ghost, albeit annoying at times, had turned out to be a real ally of his, hadn't he? Especially when it came to helping heal the rift he and Lacey had been experiencing at the time he'd popped up in Daniel's life.

'It's been so long. How *are you*?' Daniel finally exclaimed. 'And how ... well, how is it possible you're here? I thought you couldn't come back, once you'd moved on to the true afterlife?'

That's what Wilfred had told him, after all: that once you stepped through the white light that appeared for everyone after they died, there was no returning to the in-between place that you occupied while you were an, er, *ghost*.

'So how did you manage it? And how ... how's your wife? *Was* she waiting for you?'

A barrage of questions burst from Daniel's lips – there was so much he wanted to know! He did feel a beat of wariness, though, at those last couple of queries he threw Wilfred's way. The reason being, he knew the spook had missed his wife Constance terribly during the time he'd spent stuck between two worlds (she'd died quite a few years before he had); and he hadn't been sure whether there'd be a happy reunion with her, when he was finally brave enough to complete his journey to the other side.

The smile on his old friend's face softened. 'Ah. My beautiful Constance. She was indeed, boy! And being reunited with her was the most wonderful experience I've ever known.'

Daniel's heart quivered. Oh! How amazing was that to hear? He'd always wondered how Wilfred was getting on. But of course he'd had absolutely no way of finding out ... at least while he was still alive, at any rate, hah!

'So – you're happy? You've found peace?'

Wilfred nodded. 'I have, boy. I have. Or, at least,' his face scrunched into an unexpected scowl, 'I *had*. Until you decided to interrupt my idyllic afterlife, like the turnip I always knew you were!'

Daniel blinked. Er, what now? 'Hey! What's with the insults? What have *I* got to do with you coming back to your old home?'

The spook slid him a sideways look, one so full of knowing that Daniel nervously rubbed at his chin. Um. Was there something going on here, that he didn't understand? Instead of explaining what he meant by calling him a flipping turnip, though, the ghost started patting at the pockets of his jacket.

'Before we get into it, have I–? Oh. Yes. Excellent! Here we are.' Wilfred proceeded to pull out a thick cigar and a lighter. 'I *thought* I saved a little treat in here.' He lit up the cigar and took a deep drag. 'Splendid. Now, where was I–?'

'Oh, no! You can't smoke in here!' Daniel interrupted.

Wilfred raised an eyebrow. 'Steady on. You think you can tell me what to do in my own dashed house, boy?!' He took another puff of his cigar ... then, in a gesture reminiscent of his old ways, sniggered and blew the smoke right in Daniel's face.

'Hey!' Daniel coughed, before waving a panicked hand around. What would Lady Tuncaster think, if she popped her head into the shop and smelt tobacco wafting around the place? She wouldn't be amused, that was for sure. Smoking was very definitely banned from the entire hall, not just on account of all the precious antiques it housed ... but on account of it being a public space now, rather than just a family home! Thankfully – he glanced towards the shop door – the quiet morning meant he and Wilfred were, for now, still alone.

'Stop it! Put that out! Oh–'

Daniel broke off from his objections as, before him, the ghost's figure suddenly turned a little hazy, a little fuzzy around the edges. It was such a strange sight, it made him swallow nervously.

'Wilfred? Are you OK? What's going on?'

The spook put a hand to his head and groaned. A beat later, and he came fully back into focus ... but this time he had a worried look on his face. 'Oh, dear. Perhaps we ought not to bicker, old chap. I'm not sure, you see, how long I can stay here with you...'

He went on to explain.

He'd worked out that he could return to visit Daniel – but only because he was one of the few spirits in the afterlife who'd spent time tied to the earth plane after his death.

'It seems those of us who wander as lost souls for a while retain a connection to this realm,' he nodded.

A connection that meant, if they tried hard enough, and put enough energy into the endeavour, they could return to that realm – albeit for only short periods of time. How short, exactly, Wilfred wasn't quite sure – given this was the first time he'd ever attempted to temporarily vacate the afterlife.

'So,' he rued. 'Let's not waste any more time, boy. Because someone needs to bring you to your senses, what? And looking down on what's been going on in your life, I've long since realised that person was going to have to – once again, hah! – be me.'

Daniel still wasn't following. He wasn't following *at all*. What on earth could he possibly need bringing to his senses about? Had all that, er, realm-hopping affected his old mate's brain or something?!

It was interesting though, he admitted, to hear Wilfred say that those in the afterlife could look down on what was happening here on earth...

'You look confused, boy? Why does that not surprise me? I always used to say you weren't the brightest button, didn't I?' the ghost tittered.

'Hey!' Daniel's cheeks turned red. More insults? What kind of a reunion was this supposed to be?!

'Alright, alright. Dash it. Splendid sport as it is to see you getting all indignant, I suppose, I ought to get to the point.'

Wilfred took another drag of his cigar, before pointing at the sparkly Christmas tree in the middle of the shop.

'I came here, in the spirit of Christmas – 'tis the season of selflessness, after all, what? – to help you, boy. Let me explain.'

He went on to talk, of how even after he'd moved into the afterlife, he'd kept an eye on how Daniel was doing. He'd even watched him get married to Lacey, a moment that'd made him "dashed full of pride!".

That declaration had Daniel on the verge of getting misty-eyed all over again. Until, that was, he noticed the spook's face had turned sombre. So sombre, he braced himself for what was coming next...

'But you made me a promise, boy.'

'I did?'

'Indeed. The very last time I saw you, that night at the Grace Hall cemetery, you swore to me you'd be a wonderful husband to Miss T, when you finally wed—'

'She's not Miss T anymore,' Daniel interrupted. "Miss T" came from Lacey's maiden name, Thornton; and was how Wilfred had always referred to her back before they'd gotten married. 'She's *Mrs*, er, H – for Hargreaves – these days.'

The spook waved a hand. 'No need to be a nit-picker, boy. Miss T, Mrs H – you know who I'm speaking of. But the point I'm *trying* to make,' he gravely shook his head, 'is that you haven't kept your promise.'

What? Daniel felt a jolt of shock. 'My promise to be a good husband? But – of course I've kept it!' What on earth was Wilfred talking about? He was a *great* husband to Lacey! That was something he didn't have a single doubt about. He was loyal. Loved her to bits. He also did all the practical things a steadfast husband should: he had a steady job, brought money in to the household, cooked, shopped for groceries, pulled his weight with the housework. (Yes, he *knew* those last few points were areas he'd once fallen awfully short on – hence the rough patch he and Lacey had once gone through. But he'd changed his idle ways a long time ago. He'd had to, or Lacey would never have married him!)

Despite his assertions, the spook continued to shake his head.

'I'm sorry to say that, despite your good start, lately you've been anything *but* a decent husband to that poor girl. In fact, I'd say you've reverted to being quite rotten to her.' He quickly held up a finger before Daniel, whose jaw had begun to tighten in irritation, could protest further.

'Now, now, before you go getting yourself in a grump, old boy, hear me out...'

Wilfred's voice softened, then, as he explained he *knew* things in Daniel's life hadn't been going quite to plan of late.

'I *know* you're desperate to have a moppet or two of your own. I understand that. And,' his face creased in sympathy, 'I'm afraid I can't offer any assurances on whether your luck's going to change on that front. What I can say, though,' he shook his head, 'is that you need to cease your nonsense, man.

'This constant fussing and fretting you're subjecting Miss T to isn't healthy. Indeed, I declare she's a saint to tolerate it! But I have to warn you– Oh.'

The ghost went all fuzzy again. In fact, this time he half-disappeared into thin air, leaving Daniel waving his hands in panic.

He couldn't pretend he liked – or even agreed! – with what Wilfred was saying to him. His claim he wasn't a good husband was definitely off track. And what on earth did he mean about "ceasing his nonsense"?! Or that he was "fussing and fretting" over Lacey? He didn't do anything of the sort! He ... he supposed he was *a little* more involved in her day-to-day life than he used to be, if that was what Wilfred was getting at. He made nearly all her meals these days; laid out her daily fertility supplements; encouraged her to exercise; admittedly got a bit hot under the collar if she didn't get to bed early; and sent her regular reminders to drink plenty of water and not push herself too hard or get too stressed out when she was at work. But those were all *positive* things, he nodded. The actions of a kind, loving husband who just wanted his wife TO FINALLY FALL PREGNANT. That was all. In fact, all the things he did for her surely made *him* the saint, he decided defiantly. Not Lacey!

Still, despite the fact he seemed to have gotten the wrong end of the stick in regards how things were between him and Lacey, Daniel didn't want Wilfred to leave him like this. Not ... not with the words "*I have to warn you*" left hanging in the air! After all, it seemed like it had been quite an effort for the spook to have made it back to the realm of ghosts 'n ghouls. The journey had taken him away from his beloved wife, too. So whatever he was here to warn him about was probably quite significant and serious indeed, Daniel realised. The thought made him go cold all over, so much so he stared at the spook's shadowy figure and willed it to return.

Thankfully, a beat later the ghost surged back into focus. But he was grimacing, his face screwed up in concentration, as though it was taking a lot of effort to stay in the room.

'Boy. I fear my time here is nearly up. So – please! Don't be a blockhead. Just listen carefully to what I have to say.'

Daniel, grateful to see there was still a chance of hearing Wilfred's warning, quickly nodded in agreement.

'Miss T – you need to look after her, better than you've been doing. Because, dash it, old chap. I don't want to see you losing what you have ... for something you might never know. It's a gamble that's not worth taking. Do you under ... understand ... what I'm ... I'm saying ...'

The ghost's voice grew faint. His outline once again turned blurry.

Oh. 'Don't go!' Daniel yelped. He reached out, as though he could grab hold of his old friend. But all he grasped at was air. 'Please. I'm not following. What do you *mean*? About Lacey? About losing what I have–'

But it was too late. A now almost-translucent Wilfred was raising his hand in a wave. Daniel, swallowing hard, strained to hear his last words.

'*Adieu,* dear fellow. Make this a wonderful Christmas – not a wasted one...'

And then, just like that, he disappeared.

Daniel held his breath. He waited, hoping the spook might make one final return, to answer the questions suddenly clamouring in his mind.

But nothing happened.

He waited a moment more. Then he glanced around the shop and realised it felt different than it had a moment ago. It felt ... empty. Still.

Silent.

He wasn't coming back, was he? Daniel realised. A sadness slid into his heart. Especially when he thought of how he hadn't even gotten to say goodbye to his old friend.

He padded slowly across the shop and took a seat on the stool behind the counter. His head was spinning, he realised. In fact, he felt really quite dazed indeed. If it wasn't for the very-real scent of tobacco still lingering in the air, he might've wondered if he'd imagined the last few minutes altogether.

But he hadn't imagined them, had he?

He mulled over the worrying words Wilfred had left him with, twisting his fingers anxiously as he did so.

What had he *meant*? he wondered again. About losing what he had? Or that he needed to look after Lacey better? How was that even *possible*?! Given the way he was always making her lovely, healthy meals, telling her to take it easy, worrying about how she was doing? Truly, all he *did* these days was look after his wife!

He realised he was frowning so tightly, his forehead muscles were beginning to ache. But try as he might, Daniel couldn't release the tension that suddenly gripped him. How could *anyone* relax, after receiving an ominous warning from a ghostly figure?! Not just a warning of loss; a warning that he might ... might never have the one thing he was *desperate* for.

Because that's what his old friend had been getting at, wasn't it?

That he might never experience being a dad. Wilfred had said he couldn't offer him any assurances on that front. And then there'd been those parting words of his, too:

I don't want to see you losing what you have ... for something you might never know.

For something he might *never know*?

Daniel gulped, then twisted round on his stool to stare out of the window behind him. He took in the drenched gardens and barren branches of the silver birch trees scattered through the grounds.

And then he felt it. Alone in the shop, with Wilfred now gone and the wintery weather beating on outside, he was hit with a sense of hopelessness. It seemed to seep into every part of him, so intensely that suddenly all he wanted to do was hide out in the store cupboard and sob.

Sob, for everything this year *hadn't* been.

And for everything he'd just been warned *his life* might never be...

NINE

'What do you think?!'

Lacey tripped into the living room and did an impromptu twirl in front of her husband, to show off the swishy skirt of the long, open-backed black dress she was wearing. It was a lot more glamorous than the sweater 'n jeans combos she usually wore – especially given the messy bun and strappy heels she'd paired it with. She'd wanted to make an effort for tonight, though – because it wasn't every day you got to go to a Christmas Party! But that's exactly where she and Daniel were headed off to this evening: Saturday had finally come around, and it was time for the F-Group's festive fundraiser!

'What? Oh. Yeah. You look nice.'

Oh. Her husband's words were *kind*-of complimentary; but he sounded monotone, like he was depressed or something, rather than feeling – like she did – a little buzzy with anticipation for the fun night ahead.

Or, at least, she *had* felt a little buzzy, while she'd been upstairs getting ready, dance tunes beating out of her phone as she fixed her hair and brushed on some make up. Now a sense of apprehension settled over Lacey as she anxiously eyed her husband.

Despite the fact he was dressed up, too – in black trousers and a new, navy blue shirt – he was sprawled across the sofa, with the TV blaring in front of him. The way he was slouched meant his smart shirt was already creased. But she didn't care much about that. She only cared that his whole body language – from the slump of his shoulders to the downbeat look on his gorgeous face, seemed to give off the same glum vibes as his tone of voice.

It was worrying. Especially because he'd been like this all week! But she didn't know what had gotten him so down, or why he'd become so quiet, so withdrawn, in the evenings they shared together after work – because any attempt on her part to ask if he was OK, if he wanted to talk, had been met with a "*You wouldn't understand*" mutter.

So help me understand, talk to me! she'd wanted to exclaim.

Only, she hadn't done that. She couldn't *force* him to talk to her, after all. But she was worried about what was behind the strange mood her husband had fallen into, these past days.

Had something happened at Grace Hall? she'd wondered, at first. It seemed like he loved his job; and yet she'd first noticed his strange mood when he'd come home from work on Tuesday evening.

But perhaps that was a silly thought, she'd gone on to tell herself. Because it was probably *obvious* what was wrong.

He ... he was probably feeling like *she* had, when she'd been Christmas shopping with Ella. It was probably hitting him, hard, that the holiday period was coming ... and they had no baby to share it with, no baby to make the day extra sparkly and special. It was certainly an unhappy reality she found *herself* musing sadly over, too much of the time at the moment. And, yes, Daniel might have been quite relentlessly insistent they had to stay positive about their fertility journey, these past months. But no one could stay positive all the time, could they?

This battle ... it was hard, she acknowledged. She went through good days and bad days herself. On the good days, she'd remind herself they hadn't even seen a fertility specialist yet, hadn't even explored options that might change their luck, like IVF.

But on the bad days ... well. She looked at her hands. On *those* days, the sense of overwhelm, the helplessness that took hold of you, at the thought you might never become a parent, could you leave you weeping in despair. Sometimes she'd take a shower, just so she could let tears of sorrow and fear run down her face, without Daniel seeing. (Because if he witnessed her crying over their situation, you see, he'd get all frantic that her "stressed state" might affect their chance of conceiving that particular month.)

Anyway. The point was, she wouldn't wish those bad-day feelings on anybody, never mind the love of her life. So if that *was* what was driving her husband's sadness this week – and it was more than likely that it was, right? – then her heart was full of sympathy for him.

That wasn't all she felt, though. As she glanced again at his bleak face, guilt wound itself a little tighter around her tummy.

Once again, she couldn't help but beat herself up for the time she'd spent on her own personal issues around motherhood last year. Which she *knew* was pointless. But, still. Did *Daniel* think she'd hampered their chances of being parents, by wasting time looking backwards? Time they could've used to make an earlier start on trying for a little one? Did he wonder, too, if those months might have seen better quality eggs on her part, or stronger swimming sperm on his?

Since he wouldn't talk to her about what was going on in his head this week (which was frustrating because they'd promised, last year, not to hide things from one another anymore!) she really didn't know. All she *did* know, was that – as well as telling him she loved him and trying to make sure he knew she was there for him – she'd made an even bigger point than usual of showing, these past few days, her dedication to his healthy lifestyle plan. But even a week of spirulina smoothies; *and* star-jumping, squatting and sweating her way through a Full Body Cardio workout she'd found on YouTube – to prove she was working on her fitness – didn't make him smile. (That the latter didn't lift his mood had been particularly disappointing ... given she'd been left crippled with Major Muscle Soreness after all that leaping around her own living room!).

Maybe, she considered hopefully, tonight's party would cheer him up? There'd be food and drink and jolly Christmas music; plus Rob, his best mate, was coming along, as well as Olly, Ella's boyfriend, who he got on well with, too. Perhaps *their* company could lift his dejected mood ... in a way she just didn't seem able to, right now?

Since they were both avoiding alcohol on account of their health drive, they drove to the party rather than forking out for a taxi. After finding a space in one of the city centre car parks, they walked the remaining short distance to the library. When they arrived at the old building Lacey noticed her grandma – who'd treated herself to a second-hand Mini when she'd come home from her European tour last year – had actually managed to nab one of the few parking spots right outside the venue. She didn't appear to be in any rush to make her way into the party, though – not given the way she was hovering around in the lit-up forecourt, peering into her open boot.

Lacey and Daniel walked over to greet her. As they did, Lacey caught a glimpse of what was inside the trunk of her grandma's car: namely, large black bin liners, stuffed full with goodness-knew-what. Just like the one she'd been lugging around at the Christmas market last weekend.

She frowned, then – reminding herself that her grandma's life was a mystery, half the time – shrugged and tapped Rose on the arm. 'Grandma, hi! How are you? Are you excited about the party– Oh.'

She and Daniel started in unison as her grandma suddenly slammed her car boot shut.

'Hello, you nosy pair!' she clucked, whipping round to face them. 'Sneaking up on me, are you? To try and have a good old gawp into my trunk?'

Er. Lacey and Daniel shared an amused glance. And in that moment, although she was a bit confused as to *why* her grandma would be touchy about them witnessing her car boot being full of stuffed bin liners (*What was she hiding*?! she mused); that shared, wry look lifted her heart. The reason being, it made her feel connected to Daniel, in a way she realised she hadn't, for quite a while. Which was like a Christmas gift all in itself.

She reached for her husband's hand and gave it a squeeze, hoping this was going to set the tone for the rest of the night. But it seemed she was overly optimistic in that thought because, a beat later, he pulled his hand away, shoved it into his pocket, and returned to looking like he had the weight of the world on his shoulders.

As the three of them made their way into the library, Lacey bit back a worried sigh. They left their coats in the cloakroom then headed upstairs, where – thanks to the upbeat tones of Elton John's "Step Into Christmas" bouncing out of the doorway – it was obvious which room the party was being held in!

As they walked inside, Lacey blinked. Of course she'd helped in decorating the space for tonight's event. But she'd had to leave early, hadn't she? So she hadn't seen the finished result.

The place looked absolutely amazing! She glanced around, wide-eyed. Unlike the other night, the overhead lights had now been switched off, so the room was dark. It meant the reams of fairy lights they'd hung appeared extra-glittery and vibrant. The huge Christmas tree was flashing with ice-white lights, too; and everywhere she looked there was something sparkly and twinkly to catch her eye: loops of silver tinsel; dangling snowmen; shiny star ornaments. Tables and chairs were clustered around the edges of the room, so the centre could be used as a dance floor (Lacey was pretty sure the DJ was going to have everybody on their feet, with the mix of fun and festive tracks she knew was on the playlist tonight!). To one side there was also a table loaded with raffle prizes, like bottles of wine and cookery books; and, next to it, a microphone on a stand, presumably for making announcements as the night went on.

'Oh. Isn't this something special?' she breathed, feeling – despite the worries in her home life – a little thrill rush through her.

Next to her, Rose grinned in agreement. 'It is indeed, my dear.'

Lacey smiled back, then turned to look up at Daniel ... but he didn't say anything, just shrugged and sloped off in search of a – soft – drink.

Lacey watched him cross the floor, pour some orange juice into a paper cup, then slump down in a chair in a dark corner of the room. Guilt once again fizzed through her at his forlorn state. She was just about to go over and join him, to try again to get him smiling, for tonight at least ... but then a load of familiar faces from F-Group streamed through the doorway behind her, and she got caught up in a round of greetings and exclamations over how adorable all the decorations looked. And then her mum appeared in front of her, eager to say hi; along with her partner, Maz, who pulled Lacey into a warm hug.

Given his big strong arms (thanks to his job as a kickboxing instructor) Lacey always imagined Maz's hugs were like how cuddling a friendly bear would feel! Especially since he had a huge heart into the bargain. So much so that even *Sadie*, with all the scars she bore from the violence in her past, had managed to find a way of trusting his love. In fact, one of the biggest changes that'd happened since she'd begun her therapy sessions – to help deal with the events of that past – was that Sadie had taken the very brave step of finally agreeing to live with Maz, something he'd wanted to happen for a while.

Lacey was super-proud of her mum for that happy turn of events; and excited, too, for the pair, given it meant this Christmas would be their very first shared under the same roof together! That thought made her hug Maz a little tighter, in gratitude for how he'd brought such goodness into Sadie's life.

After that, more people began to arrive. The fleece-wearing ladies from F-Group appeared en-masse (Lacey noticed, wryly, that they'd swapped their usual zip-up tops for jaunty Christmas jumpers and dangly, Christmas-bauble-shaped earrings). Couples filed in through the door, too; plus family groups, including kids – wearing reindeer ears and sparkly shoes – who immediately ran over to inspect the cling-film-wrapped buffet at the back of the room.

And then Charlotte and Cooper appeared. As she pressed a kiss to her cheek, Lacey realised Charlotte smelt divine – like a decadent mix of jasmine and vanilla. Her mate *looked* stunning, too, in a long-sleeved, figure-hugging red dress that matched her scarlet nails, something she made sure to tell her.

'Aw, you look super-cute too, honey,' Charlotte replied. 'I love that dress you're wearing. It's so sultry! And check out your waistline!' She slipped her hands around Lacey's waist, then pulled a mock-jealous pout. 'Hey, since when did you get so tiny?! I suppose you're always rocking sweaters at work – they *definitely* don't show off your figure like this slip-of-a-dress does!'

Lacey found herself blushing at the compliment. Her mate's words weren't something she'd been expecting to hear – especially when it seemed she hadn't exactly wowed her own husband with the effort she'd tried to put into her appearance tonight!

She noticed Hazel and Neville appear in the doorway, and she excused herself to go over and greet them. Hazel looked pretty in pink lipstick and a frilly fuchsia dress, and the couple were holding hands, which was *soo* cute it made Lacey's heart melt!

A few more familiar faces strolled in behind them: Daniel's best mate Rob, and his girlfriend Abby, who were excited to be on a night out (their little boy Milo was being watched by Abby's sister); plus Ella and Olly (in their case, Lina was in the care of her doting grandmother, Olly's mum!).

Rob and Olly went off to find Daniel; while Lacey, Ella, Charlotte and Abby gathered in a huddle and chatted animatedly, about one another's outfits and their plans for the holiday season ahead. Then, when the room was finally full to the brim with guests – all chattering and fetching drinks and bobbing their heads to the tunes thumping out of the speaker system – F-Group's Sheila took to the mic to give a little *Welcome-and-thanks-for-coming*! speech. She also asked for people to try and buy as many raffle tickets as they could manage: "It's all for a good cause, remember!".

Everyone clapped and cheered, and then, with the party officially started, the DJ took over once more. As the notes of Wizzard's enduringly-popular "I Wish it Could be Christmas Everyday" filled the air, Lacey found herself being tugged towards the dance floor by Rose, who wanted to have a boogie with her granddaughter. The rest of the girls joined them, and the next hour or so passed in a blur of shimmying and giggling under the flashing disco ball.

Eventually, it was announced the buffet was opening, and the music quietened down as everyone made a beeline for the tables that were crammed with all sorts of party food: squishy, sticky cream cakes that had been donated by a local bakery; cheese 'n pickle sticks; quiches and sausage rolls; endless varieties of crisps.

As they lined up to browse the offerings, Lacey noticed, wryly, that her grandma – paper plate at the ready – had somehow managed to position herself at the head of the buffet queue. Why didn't that surprise her? she laughed. Rose was always good for sniffing out the grub on offer at *any* event (and happily admitted half the reason she attended the weekly F-Group meetings was simply for the free coffee and biscuits!).

When it was her turn to fill her plate, though, Lacey's happy mood melted away a little. After all, all the slices of pizza and plates of mince pies and bowls of gummy sweets on offer *looked* super-scrummy; but they definitely weren't healthy. For a moment she felt a beat of panic: was there *anything* she could have? she gulped, eyes flitting left and right. She didn't want people to think she was being fussy, but she also couldn't risk letting Daniel see her with something processed or full of sugar, and make him feel even more despondent this evening. Thankfully, she managed to locate some cucumber sticks and grapes, plus a few plain crackers and a spoonful or two of couscous salad. And when Ella gave her a funny look and pointed out there were chocolate-covered donuts on offer – which she knew Lacey loved – Lacey shot a nervous glance in her husband's direction and fibbed that "she wasn't all that hungry right now".

Happy sounds filled the room as people congregated at the tables or hovered near the buffet, and ate and drank and gossiped. Lacey noticed, across the table *she* was sitting at (she and Rose and the girls had finally joined the boys at the back of the room), that Daniel had chosen a similar selection of foodstuffs as she had. She caught his eye and tried to give him a "look-at-us-being-so-good!" wry smile, but he just shrugged and gloomily slung a cucumber stick in his mouth. So she swallowed then turned back to Ella, who was recounting an adorable story about Lina; and of how the little girl's mouth had dropped open in astonishment when she'd first seen the glittering Christmas tree her parents had set up in their living room that week!

Not long after that Rose, who was sitting to Lacey's right, shoved down what was left of her buffet haul – a handful of sweet chilli crisps – then brushed the crumbs off her lap and stood up. Lacey didn't bother asking where she was going ... because she had a pretty good idea her grandma would be heading straight back to the food area to help herself to seconds! So she was surprised to notice that, instead of returning to see what other cakes and goodies were on offer that she'd yet to try, Rose slipped out of the room altogether.

Maybe she was just heading for the bathroom, Lacey shrugged, not giving her disappearance another thought. Until, that was, a good twenty minutes or so later, when Rose finally reappeared at their table, looking slightly breathless and with vivid pink cheeks, like she'd been out in the cold.

'Grandma? Are you OK? Where've you been?!'

Rose looked delighted by that question, given the way her rheumy eyes twinkled. And yet all she offered in way of an answer was: 'Hah. You'll see – soon enough!'

They were interrupted, then, by someone tapping the microphone at the front of the room. Lacey turned her head, realising that someone was actually her mum, who wanted to say a few words to everybody.

The room obliging quietened down as Sadie thanked everyone again for coming along tonight, and for their support towards The Cocoon refuge for women and children.

'Christmas is a happy time of year for many. But not for everyone,' she went on to say, her voice grave.

She explained further: every year during the festive season, the refuge saw a sad increase in the number of domestic abuse victims needing help. The stress of the holiday period; money worries; increased alcohol intake over Christmas – all of those things played a part in the escalating violence they saw each December, and into the New Year. It was a bitter truth that left a dark stain on what was supposed to be a time of goodwill and benevolence.

Sadie's voice grew passionate as she outlined those facts. So passionate, Lacey braced herself, wondering if her mum was going to get angry and start snarling into the microphone. It was a topic, after all, that had *always* got her riled up in the past. (And quite understandably so, Lacey nodded; but there was a time and a place for that anger to emerge, and a fun fundraiser probably wasn't it – they wanted people to support similar events in future, not give them a wide berth because they were nervous of the host!)

It turned out she needn't have worried, though, because her mum seemed to realise she was becoming awfully animated – and she did something Lacey hadn't seen her do before.

She paused. Took a visible deep breath. And then ... well then she told the room to give themselves a round of applause!

'By being here and supporting this event, you're not only ensuring we can continue providing a safe space for survivors, as they rebuild their lives. You're also showing that you *care*. That you understand what lies at the heart of Christmas. This time of year is not just about Buck's fizz and buying gifts. It's also about sparing some time to think of the less fortunate. So – thank you. And Happy Holidays!'

Oh, what a lovely speech! The room whistled and cheered and Lacey, filled with pride for her mum, joined in, clapping so hard her hands stung.

Sadie beamed out at the crowd. She was just about to hand back over to the DJ – it was surely time for more dancing! – when Rose suddenly stood up and hurried over to take the microphone from her hand.

'Wait, wait. I've a little something I'd like to announce, too...'

Sadie looked at her mother in surprise, but obliging handed over the mic.

'Maz? Daniel? Are you there?' Rose held a hand over her eyes as she peered into the depths of the room. 'Come and give me a hand, would you, my dears?'

Across the table Daniel shot Lacey a puzzled look but did as he was asked by his grandmother-in-law. He looked a little shy as he went up to stand in front of everyone, which made Lacey's heart flip – aw, bless! – even as she wondered what was going on.

Maz joined him, and Rose covered the microphone as she whispered instructions in their ears.

The next thing everyone knew, the two men were scrambling behind the large Christmas tree – only to emerge with *big black bin liners*, stuffed to the brim with goodness-knew-what, clamped in their hands! They each tipped one of the bags onto the floor ... and the room strained their necks as one to see what tumbled out.

Toys. That's what spilled out from the bags. Toys of every description: jigsaws and board games, colouring books and crayons, baby dolls, pots of Play-Doh, model dinosaurs, mini racing cars.

Rose waved at the colourful items lining the floor.

'It can't be a pleasant experience at any time of the year, for a child to have to spend time at a domestic violence shelter. But how especially unfair at Christmas!' she exclaimed. 'So, I decided I wanted to do something about that...'

She went on to say how, over the past few weeks, she'd been wandering the city centre, going from store to store to gather donations for the children at The Cocoon. Donations she hoped would soften the experience of having to spend their holidays in a strange environment, away from the homes they'd known.

'This is the end result!' She waved at the bags full of toys then explained how no-one had noticed her heaving them in from the car just now ... because everyone had been too busy stuffing their faces with food!

The room laughed as one, and a few people called out sweet remarks, like "Well done!" and "Good on you, love!". Rose grinned, took a little bow, then made a show of peering at the still-heaving-with-goodies buffet table.

'I hope you lot haven't scoffed *all* the cakes while I was busy, though,' she mock-scolded. 'Because I think I've earned second helpings, don't you?!'

Everyone cheered at that. And then, with feel-good vibes spreading through the room, Lacey got to her feet and hurried over to hug her grandma. Oh! She felt really quite emotional at the gorgeous gesture Rose had made this evening; what a lovely, kind thing of her grandma to do! To think, she'd been gathering these toys the day she and Ella had bumped into her at the Christmas market, yet neither of them had had a clue what she'd been up to!

With the speeches finally over, the DJ started up again. This time, though, instead of chirpy Christmas music, it was a slow, lovey-dovey song that twinkled out of the speakers. In response, one by one, couples began to fill the dance floor: most Lacey didn't recognise, but she did see Hazel and Neville, smiling at one another underneath the flickering disco ball; Ella, pressing her head against Olly's chest as they swayed gently to the music; Charlotte and Cooper, standing super-close, arms wrapped around one another, the very picture of besotted-ness.

Watching alone, from the edge of the room – her grandma had gone off to indulge in those second helpings she'd talked of – Lacey felt a beat of envy. She couldn't help it. It was hard to see everyone looking so loved up, when her own husband had barely said a word to her all evening. She chewed at her lip and wished Daniel would whisk *her* onto the dance floor. Would hold her tightly, the way he used to. Like she was precious, his only love. The same way he was *her* one-and-only, and always would be.

She turned to look for him, and found he'd finished tidying away all the toys scattered over the floor. Now, he was loitering by the Christmas tree, eyes also on the swaying couples. She hesitated then started towards him, hoping that – maybe, just maybe – the upbeat vibes and happy atmosphere of the evening might finally have lifted his earlier sad mood.

She took a step towards him. Then another. He turned, saw her coming, and smiled. Just a tiny, lopsided, reluctant sort-of-a-smile, admittedly. But it was better than no smile at all, Lacey breathed. She upped her pace, keen to reach him – desperate, even, she rued, after the withdrawn demeanour he'd been rocking all week – to soak up any scrap of affection he might throw her way. To grab hold of any little sign that might show he *was* still happy to be married to her, despite their childless-status. Because, of course, that was a worry that was still hounding her heart...

As she started hurrying across the floor, though, something happened.

Her head ... it began feeling woozy. Not just woozy: dizzy. The same way, Lacey realised, she'd felt the other night when she'd been helping decorate this very hall. The same way she'd felt, too, after jogging through the field after Daniel on Sunday.

But then she realised she'd been mistaken. This *wasn't* the same as those other occasions. It was worse. Because ... because now her head was starting to pound, into the bargain.

Pound and throb and spin, so badly that the sounds of the room around her faded away, until all she could hear was a sickening, whooshing noise filling her ears.

She swallowed. Stopped in her tracks and clamped her hands to her head.
Oh, God. This wasn't nice. This wasn't nice *at all.* What was happening?
Please stop this, she begged her body.
But the sensations didn't stop. They just got worse.
Nausea filled her gut. Speckles blurred her vision. And then her legs turned wobbly. So wobbly, she found herself blindly flailing around, hoping to find a stray chair or something she could grab onto and use to regain her balance.

Her hands met with nothing but air.
A heartbeat later ... Lacey's world went black.

TEN

'Oh my God. Lacey? Someone get help! Please. Quickly!'
Oh.
Oh *man*. Lacey, groggy, blinked. For a moment she didn't have a clue what was happening. And then she realised she ... she was in Daniel's arms. How did she get there? And why was he looking down at her, with his eyes wide in shock?

'Lacey? *Lacey*?! Are you OK?' He turned away, to address someone she couldn't see. 'I think she's coming round.'

'Lay her flat. We need to raise her legs.'

That was her mum's voice, Lacey realised. And then she felt herself being gently laid on the cold wooden floor. Something soft was tucked under her head, and then someone lifted her legs and slid a cushion – or something similarly squishy – underneath them, too.

'What's happening– Oh. *Bleugh*.' She tried to talk, but felt so sickly and awful, like she could just vomit her guts up, that it was hard to do anything but groan.

'Don't try and talk. Just lay still. You passed out,' Sadie told her.

She passed out? Oh. But of course. As Lacey looked up, to see her mum had joined Daniel in hovering over her, she suddenly recalled how dizzy and nauseous she'd felt, before everything had gone black. How embarrassing, though, to collapse in front of everybody!

She tried again to get up, conscious that the music seemed to have been turned down and that more people had begun hovering around her, their faces taut with worry: Ella, Rose, Charlotte, Maz.

'Is she alright?'; 'Has someone called an ambulance?'; 'You know – I *thought* she looked awfully pale tonight.'

Voices murmured around her, concerned, and Lacey felt like a right party-pooper for interrupting everyone's night.

'I'm OK. It was just a funny turn,' she tried to tell them all. And then, even though she still felt pretty yucky, she made a move to sit up, ready to put on a brave face so people could get back to enjoying their evening out. But her mum put a firm hand on her shoulder and told her to stay put.

'Oh, no. You're not going anywhere. Not until you've been checked over. The paramedics are on their way.'

'But–'

'Your mum's right. Please, Lacey. Just lie still. I ... I couldn't handle it if you passed out again,' Daniel chipped in, his voice shaking.

Lacey looked at him, surprised to hear such emotion in his voice.

'By the way,' Sadie patted him on the shoulder, and Lacey noticed her face was filled with gratitude, the likes of which she'd never seen her mum direct towards her husband before. 'Good catch. I've never seen anyone move as quickly as you did just now. She went down so fast, she could've smashed her head on the floor. You saved her. Well done,' she nodded. 'Really well done.'

Daniel's cheeks turned pink. Then he looked back at Lacey and stroked her hair, and all she could think was: she'd ended up in her husband's arms just now ... because he'd dived to catch her as she fell??

Oh. Well, that was romantic. Right? Baby or not, that showed he still cared about her. Didn't it?

Didn't it?

She really hoped so.

The green-uniformed paramedics – a female and a male, whose name badges declared them to be Chaaya and Toby, respectively – arrived a short time later. While they slowly sat Lacey up and proceeded to run a few tests on her, the party resumed in the background, albeit on a slightly quieter note.

'Has this happened before?' Chaaya asked, as she attached a blood pressure cuff to Lacey's arm. Lacey knew she had to tell her the truth. Which was that, she might not have passed out before; but this wasn't the first dizzy spell she'd had lately, was it? When she divulged as much, though, Daniel looked really quite horrified; and her mum, too, went a bit pale. They didn't say anything, though, clearly not wanting to interrupt the paramedics as they went through their observations.

Eventually, after pricking her finger to test her glucose levels, Chaaya nodded sagely.

'Everything else looks good. But your blood sugar's *definitely* too low. That could explain why you fainted.' She looked carefully at Lacey. 'You look quite thin. Have you been restricting what you've been eating?'

Um. For a moment, Lacey wasn't quite sure how to answer that. Of course she hadn't been *restricting* her eating as such. But: 'We ... we're trying for a baby. We have been, for quite a while actually. The doctor told us a healthy lifestyle was important,' she explained hesitantly. 'So I have tried to cut out all the junk and sugary stuff lately.'

Chaaya and Toby exchanged a look.

'So what *have* you been eating?' Toby asked, gently.

'Lots of good stuff,' she answered quickly, feeling Daniel's eyes on her. 'You know – fruits and veggies. Brown rice. Lentils. Quinoa. That's all really, um, nutritious. Right?'

Once again, the paramedics looked at one another. And then Chaaya nodded and patted Lacey's arm.

'Trying for a baby? That's a really huge deal,' she nodded, sympathy shining in her deep brown eyes. 'But – given you've had a few dizzy spells – I suspect you might be overdoing things. It's good to eat well, but I don't think you're eating *enough*. And running around with a low blood sugar definitely isn't healthy. You need to be strong, to conceive a child. You need to support your body. Do you understand?

'Now. We need to get some food in you before we go, to get your blood sugar back to a safe level.' Chaaya eyed the buffet at the side of the room, and Sadie quickly scrambled to her feet.

'I'll fetch her some options. What's best?'

'Something substantial,' Toby advised. 'Some fruit juice or a sugary drink, for starters. And then some sandwiches, quiche, something like that. A big slice of cake would be great, too – looks like you've got plenty yummy-looking options over there!'

What? No! She couldn't eat stuff like that! Not unless she *really* wanted to throw her poor husband over the edge, Lacey gulped.

'No. Please. If I have to eat something, I'll just have some fruit. There's a big bowl of grapes. And maybe a bit more couscous salad.'

But it seemed like no one was listening to her, because the next thing she knew – and while the paramedics were tidying away their equipment – her mum plonked a heaving plate of food on her lap.

It contained a handful of sandwiches. Crisps. A couple of sausage rolls. Salted peanuts. And a ... a big hunk of what looked like chocolate fudge cake.

Everything looked *really* good. So good, her mouth began to water...

But then she felt Daniel's eyes on her and quickly shook her head.

'I'm sorry. I can't eat this. It's not healthy *at all*.' Deep down, Lacey had a horrible feeling that Chaaya was right: that the light-headedness she'd been experiencing was a sign she wasn't keeping herself as strong as she should. Yet she still uttered the words she knew Daniel would want her to. Her guilt over running him around last year on the baby-topic was too intense to be overruled, you see. And since he really believed – especially given their "unexplained" infertility status – that clean living was going to be the magic key in bringing a little one into their lives, she had to support him on that, whatever it took.

She was the one person in the world, after all, who saw the fear and frustration in his eyes, every single month, when yet another waste-of-money pregnancy test showed a negative result.

She understood what their situation was doing to him. Understood he was becoming more and more panicked that he might *never* get to be a dad. She could feel that torment, hovering around him, every single day. It was why he'd been so downbeat all this week, she was sure of it. And it was why he was so driven with this whole healthy-lifestyle issue. Why he was fighting so hard. Why he needed *her* to fight so hard, too.

Of course, if you hadn't experienced the banging-your-head-against-a-wall exasperation and unfairness of infertility ("Why won't something that's supposedly so natural just happen for us, when it seems to happen so easily

FOR EVERYBODY ELSE?!"), then you couldn't understand the lengths a person might go to to change their luck. If you'd never woken in the dead of night, with the cold realisation you might *never* get to have a child of your own seeping into your heart; if you'd never had bitter tears running down your crumpled face as you wondered just how on earth you were going to survive that truth, then you might *sympathise*. But you couldn't understand. Not truly.

But *she* understood what Daniel was feeling ... because she was feeling all those same things, too.

Her mum blinked. 'Lacey? What are you talking about? You *have* to eat. The medics have just told you that.'

'Then get me something healthy! If I put this stuff into my body I might mess up my ovulation or my hormones might get out of synch or–'

She sounded half-crazed, Lacey knew, as she ranted on. But Daniel was looking at her, staring at her, willing her, she was sure, to stay strong. To keep to the programme. She couldn't let him down. Not again.

'Lacey.' Suddenly, his hand was on her shoulder.

She broke off from her panicked outburst to glance nervously up at him. 'I'm sorry. I can't believe I fainted like that! I'll look after myself better in future. I promise I will. Don't be mad with me.'

'Mad? Why the heck would he be *mad* at you?' Sadie frowned and looked between them. And in that moment Lacey saw something on her mum's face that she hadn't seen in a while.

Suspicion.

Her eyes narrowed as she stared at her son-in-law. The son-in-law she'd, for the longest time, been convinced would hurt her daughter...

Daniel must have sensed the change in Sadie's mood, too, because he swallowed. And then, quickly, he shook his head.

'I'm not mad at you! I can't even believe you'd think that. Al ... although–' His voice cracked. He looked away for a second. When he looked back at her, Lacey noticed tears in his eyes.

'Please, eat what your mum's brought you. Everyone's right. You *do* need to be strong. I–'

It seemed like he was going to say something else, but he broke off and simply waved at her plate. And Chaaya looked up from where she was gathering her equipment together and noted, gently, that they couldn't leave until Lacey's blood sugar had improved...

And so Lacey found herself doing what should've been the simplest thing in the world. She ate the plate of food in front of her ... but felt riddled with guilt at every bite.

ELEVEN

Back at the gift shop on Monday morning, and Daniel felt like all the cheery, festive, sparkly items on the shelving units – from the spiced-apple scented candles, to the shimmering angel tree-toppers – were mocking him.

Because this December was getting more woeful by the day, wasn't it?

He walked to one of the sash windows and stared at the grey skies outside. Then he sighed, pressed his forehead against the cool glass and let his thoughts run back over everything that'd happened these past few days.

Firstly, there'd been his unexpected reunion with Wilfred. Seeing his old friend pop up out of the blue like that had been a shock, that was for sure! And although it had been great to know the spook was doing OK, that he was happy and reunited with his wife, out there in the true afterlife, Daniel couldn't pretend the words Wilfred had left him with had been easy to deal with. In fact, they'd whirred round in his mind on an almost-continuous loop for the rest of that week:

I know you're desperate to have a moppet or two of your own; I'm afraid I can't offer any assurances on whether your luck's going to change on that front.

This constant fussing and fretting you're subjecting Miss T to isn't healthy.

I don't want to see you losing what you have ... for something you might never know.

Day by day he'd stewed over those remarks, until he'd felt so worn down and despondent, even Lacey's worried glances and attempts at loving hugs – attempts he'd brushed off – hadn't been able to lift his mood.

Not to say he didn't feel bad for the way he'd been so aloof with her lately. He did. But he'd simply felt too lost in his own world, last week, to let her in. After all, it wasn't like he could share the experience he'd gone through. He couldn't exactly admit he'd been visited by a long-dead, hoity-toity former Earl of Grace Hall, and been left with sobering words ringing in his ears, now, could he?!

It was particularly the *"something you might never know"* statement that'd affected him, Daniel knew ... seeing how that clearly referred to the chance of him having a baby of his own. The other remarks Wilfred had made – about him not living up to his promise of being a great husband to Lacey – although annoying, hadn't bothered him *quite* so much. After all, they weren't true! he'd stubbornly told himself, over and over. Or, at least, he *had* – until the events of Saturday night...

To be honest, he hadn't much felt like going along to the F-Group Christmas party in the first place. Had only done so because he hadn't wanted to let his wife down. And during the evening it had been hard to pretend he'd been having a good time, like everyone around him. Like his mates Rob and

Olly, who'd been laughing and drinking and even let themselves be dragged to the dance floor once or twice by their other halves.

But then the night had taken a turn in a direction he *really* hadn't seen coming...

Daniel's tummy flipped as he recalled the moment he'd realised something was wrong with Lacey. She'd been coming towards him, round the edge of the dance floor. And even though he'd still been in a dejected mood, he remembered he'd reluctantly sent a small smile her way.

It was a smile she hadn't returned. Instead, she'd stopped dead in her tracks. A confused look had come over her pretty face. She'd turned pale, too. At which point something – call it a sixth sense perhaps – had told him what was coming.

He'd lunged forward, covering the short distance between them just in time to catch her as her legs gave way underneath her.

He shuddered, still distressed by that awful moment. Of course he knew *now* that Lacey had simply fainted. That she was fine. But he hadn't known she'd be OK, during the short time he'd held her limp body in his arms.

All he'd known was– Oh! He rubbed roughly at his eyes, feeling them well up.

All he'd known, he gulped, was that his heart had nearly stopped beating, so horrified had he been at the sight of his beloved wife, out cold before him.

His face crumpled at the memory.

That still hadn't been the worst part of the night, though, he reminded himself...

Images flashed in his mind. Images of the nervous glances Lacey had sent his way after she'd come round, and the paramedics had told her her low blood sugar was to blame for the way she'd passed out. Those nervous glances had continued, when her mum had brought her a plate of food to eat from the buffet. In fact, they'd even been there the next day, when a worried Sadie had brought a hearty meal of vegetable lasagne, garlic bread and a fat strawberry cheesecake to the cottage. She'd been determined to make sure her daughter got some more decent calories into her after her woozy spell – but Lacey had seemed almost fearful of the way *he* might react to her sitting down to such a substantial Sunday lunch.

Her wariness had confused him. Even more so when he recalled the awful thing she'd said to him, after her collapse at the party: she'd pleaded with him not to be mad at her, hadn't she? But ... why on earth would she think he'd be *mad* with her, for having a funny turn??

Anyway. All those things – his wife's fainting episode; the paramedics' assertion she hadn't been eating enough; her uneasy demeanour around him; *and* Wilfred's ominous words, about how he hadn't been treating Lacey the way a good husband should – had played on his mind for the rest of the afternoon.

And then—

Daniel bit his lip. Moved away from the window and took a seat back behind the shop counter. As he twisted from side to side on his stool, he reflected on the fact there was still *one more thing* that'd happened at the weekend, to add to his worries about Lacey...

After Sadie had gone home, and the afternoon had slipped into evening, his wife had decided to take a bath.

'I can't seem to warm up,' she'd complained, making him think of how she'd also felt the cold more than he would've expected her to, at the start of their walk last Sunday. 'Maybe a long, hot soak will help.'

Worried that a slick bathtub, plus a person who'd been suffering from light-headedness, wasn't an ideal combination, Daniel had told her to call him when she was finished. The last thing anyone needed was for her to come over all dizzy again, then slip on some soap suds and hit her head on the tiled floor on her way out of the bath.

So, when she'd finished having a nice soak in lots of scented bubbles, she'd done exactly that. But when he'd walked into the well-lit bathroom and helped her step out of the tub, he'd been a bit startled by what he'd seen.

The female paramedic had said Lacey looked "quite thin", hadn't she? Well. Eyeing his wife's naked body before she could reach for her towel, Daniel noticed she'd been right. Lacey *did* look thin. Much thinner than she used to. He'd actually felt a little panicked to see the way her collarbones seemed to jut out from the base of her neck, and the sharpness of her hipbones. No wonder she'd been feeling the cold! Plus, with no make-up on, he also couldn't miss how pale and drawn she looked, or the dark circles smudged under her eyes.

She didn't look like herself at all. Why hadn't he noticed that earlier?!

As she dried herself off, he tried to tell himself it was hard to see someone's true figure in the middle of winter, when everybody was sporting big chunky jumpers on account of the freezing temperatures. That that made it perfectly understandable he hadn't noticed Lacey's weight loss. On the other hand, though – he was her flipping husband! He saw her without clothes on, on a regular basis. So surely he *should've* noticed the changes that were going on, right under his nose?

It was only then that Daniel had been hit with another realisation.

A realisation that had made him hang his head. Because – awful though it sounded – he supposed he really hadn't paid much attention to his wife *at all*, lately. And he didn't just mean on a day-to-day basis; he meant in the other ways a man should notice his wife, when they were alone together under the duvet. Sex, he admitted, had become – for him at least – nothing more than a biological act. A determined attempt to get sperm travelling up his wife's fallopian tubes, and nothing more. It certainly hadn't been passionate. He'd barely even looked at Lacey's body. And he most definitely hadn't held her close, or taken the time to kiss her tenderly, in all the places she loved to be kissed, for quite some time now...

Did that happen to other couples who were trying for a baby that wouldn't come? he wondered. Even if it did, his heart had sunk at the realisation of how ... how *distant*, he concluded, he'd become from his wife.

It wasn't right. She didn't deserve such standoffishness. And, to think, they used to be so in love. What had happened?!

By the time he'd retreated to bed, Daniel had been left feeling really quite sick indeed, at recognising – quietly, insidiously – something had gone very wrong in his marriage.

It was only as he'd been lying in the darkness, though, haunted by his thoughts, that one more remark Wilfred had made to him last week popped into his mind.

And it was a thought that suddenly made *everything* crystal clear to Daniel, as to how they'd ended up in this place.

Miss T – you need to look after her ... better than you've been doing.

That's what had gone wrong.

Moments after those words burst through his brain, Daniel propelled himself out of bed. The reason being, he suddenly felt too agitated to lie there, pretending to be asleep. Leaving Lacey slumbering on, he headed downstairs and paced the living room floor.

With every step he took, the nausea in his gut grew stronger.

Because Wilfred was correct. He ... he hadn't been looking after Lacey. He'd thought he was ... but, in truth, he'd actually been doing quite the opposite, hadn't he? Until she'd keeled over on Saturday night, though, he hadn't wanted to see that. Hadn't wanted to believe his old friend's words of warning. Had wanted to stick with the lie that all the things he was encouraging her to do in her life, were *good* for her.

But now he considered it ... how was asking Lacey to restrict what she ate, until she passed out from low blood sugar, *good for her*?! How was telling her she shouldn't eat sugar, or dairy products, or oil, for fear (on the basis of some vague articles on Google) they might do something bad to her hormones, *good for her*? How was being annoyed at her coming home late the night she'd helped with the F-Group party decorations, *good for her*? How was forcing her to watch that *How Babies are Born* TV programme *good for her*, when he knew – could see on her face! – that it upset her? And how ... how was making her flipping run through a frozen field, then scolding her for not being "cardio fit" when she got red-faced and out of breath, *good for her*?!

He gulped and pressed his hands to his face, as all those memories of the past weeks and months hit him like a tidal wave. Oh, man. What had he turned into? Why had he started to behave like the naffest husband on the planet? And why had his wife put up with him being so ... so *bossy*?!

Maybe, he thought sadly, because being the sweetheart she was, she could see he'd only ever meant well. Had only asked all those things of her, in the hope they would lead to better health ... and that that, in turn, might lead to their finally falling pregnant.

But it had all gone wrong, hadn't it? At circa 12.45am, right there in his living room, Daniel finally realised the healthy lifestyle he'd been aiming for had taken a sinister turn. He'd become too obsessive, hadn't he? Had pushed poor Lacey too far. Her weight loss, dizzy spells, drawn face, anxious demeanour around him: the evidence was damning.

It had to stop. He had to fix this. Of course he wanted to be a dad. So badly. But...

I don't want to see you losing what you have ... for something you might never know.

But he'd never wanted to hurt Lacey, or what they had, in the process. That had *never* been remotely his intention...

Back in the shop, Daniel stopped twisting from side to side on his stool, and took a deep breath. He thought again of all the wide-eyed, apprehensive looks his wife had sent his way over the weekend, and felt his heart quiver with regret.

OK. He'd spent enough time ruminating over what had gone wrong between him and Lacey. He'd barely slept last night on account of his fretting.

Now, he had to put his energy to better use. He had to think. Think of how he could put things right. Reverse what he'd done. Of how he could help Lacey feel better, and return to full strength. Of how he could look after her better in the future, just like Wilfred had told him he needed to do.

Most importantly of all, though, he nodded – he had to find a way to earn back her trust...

TWELVE

Those thoughts, of how to reverse the distance that'd grown between him and Lacey these past months; *and* of how to make her feel better and healthier, into the bargain (ideally ASAP, because he never wanted to have paramedics picking her off the floor again), dominated Daniel's brain through the rest of the morning, and into his lunch break.

A few ideas came to mind as he sat in the staff kitchen: they should have a talk, that was for sure. Re-group. He needed to apologise for pushing her so hard, lately. Maybe he could do that over a nice meal out somewhere? Or would going to a restaurant be too fraught for both of them? After all, he thought ruefully, he very clearly remembered that the *last time* they'd eaten out together, he'd cajoled his wife into ordering a dressing-free beetroot salad and a dairy-free spinach smoothie, because he'd been too nervous of how much fat or salt might have been in any of the more delicious-sounding items on the menu. He also recalled that, throughout that lunch, Lacey had constantly slid wistful glances at the neighbouring table, where a couple had been munching on burgers 'n fries 'n sticky ketchup. Yes. He remembered *that* part of their lunch date really quite well indeed... because he'd been annoyed by the look of longing all over her face!

The memory made him cringe. Seriously. What kind of a husband behaved like that?! Since when had he thought it OK to police his wife's lifestyle choices?! And how on earth had he not realised he was taking things too far? he scolded himself all over again.

Of course, he wasn't going to suggest to Lacey that they simply abandon their healthy routines completely. Dr Rhines had been quite clear that – for anybody – being in good shape was important to both conceiving *and* in having a healthy pregnancy, should you be lucky enough to end up in that happy place.

But there was healthy ... and there was *hysterical*, he lamented.

And no-one was going to fall pregnant if they weren't strong and sustained...

By the time he'd eaten his sandwiches, Daniel was feeling quite fed up with himself indeed. And really quite uninspired, too, when it came to thinking of a grand idea as to how to mend things between him and Lacey. A meal out, even at a lovely restaurant; a talk; maybe a big bouquet of wintery lilies. Those things were nice. But they were also quite routine. Not special enough to make up for his overbearing behaviour of late. Not special enough to really remind Lacey of how much he loved her.

Because he really did. In fact, as he tripped back across the gravel drive to the gift shop, in readiness for his afternoon shift, his heart ached and twisted in regret for these past months. For all the moments of panic and impatience and downright irritation he'd unfairly felt towards his wife, simply because he was Majorly Stressed Out by their lack-of-a-baby status.

He shouldn't have been taking that out on her. They were supposed to be on the same side here!

He shook his head, disappointed in himself. Then he opened the rear door to the hall and headed back inside. Just as he was walking towards the gift shop, though, something caught his eye: a little way ahead of him, a white flash burst through the air.

Daniel started. What on earth was *that*?

And then he heard a giggle. Not the same loud, Lady-Tuncaster-peal-of-laughter of the other week. This was different. This was like ... well, like a little girl's giggle.

He hesitated, just long enough to feel a ripple of glacial air snake round the back of his neck.

Oh! He shivered, then glanced back to check he'd closed the rear door of the hall properly, and that the freezing December air wasn't drifting in behind him.

The big wooden door was shut and secure.

Daniel warily returned his gaze to the long hallway in front of him.

Another flash of white shimmered before him. And then his head turned all woozy. Just the same way it had *last* week, when–

When Wilfred had made his unexpected appearance in the gift shop, to warn Daniel that his demanding ways were spoiling the promise he'd made, to be a good husband to Lacey.

Despite the funny feeling in his head, Daniel felt a flash of hope. Had his old friend gathered enough energy together to return and visit him once more? Was he, this time – just as he'd done a couple of years ago – going to give him some *practical* advice on how to put things right with Lacey? Well, wouldn't *that* be helpful?! he nodded eagerly. He knew he'd be able to trust any suggestion Wilfred made, after all – because his instincts last time he and Lacey had hit a rough patch, and what needed to be done to remedy it, had been spot on...

A beat later, though – after another giggle hit his ears – Daniel realised he was probably mistaken to think this strange pearly light could have anything to do with his old friend. Because plenty of sniggers and snickers had left Wilfred's lips during the time Daniel had known him ... but never a playful, girly *giggle*.

He knew someone else, though, who'd once laughed that way...

His eyes widened as he continued to stare down the long corridor.

Surely, this couldn't be–?

He swallowed, uncertain. Then, noticing the white light had shifted from a flash, to something more fluttery and soft and constant, he began walking slowly towards it. It seemed to sense his presence growing closer, because it giggled again, then danced off. From doorway to doorway it flit, as though drawing him along the passageway.

It wasn't long before they reached the inner hallway, where the main staircase was located. There, Daniel found himself following the light all the way up to the Persian-rug-'n-antique-armchair-adorned first floor landing. There were decadent bedrooms leading off from this area: rooms full of four-poster beds, silk curtains and original 18th century wallpaper, from which he could hear the faint murmur of visitors' voices emanating as they wandered around, taking in the sights the building had to offer.

The light didn't head towards any of those pretty spaces, though. Instead, it dashed towards the East Wing of the building, and his heart started hammering in his chest as he realised where they seemed to be headed.

He walked carefully down the narrow corridor that unfolded before him, knowing that this route led to a less grand part of the house. To the smaller, darker rooms that made up the former Nursery Wing of Grace Hall.

It was a part of the building Daniel hadn't set foot in in quite some time.

He hadn't *wanted* to. Not given the memories this area triggered in him...

He gulped but walked on, until he saw the light dart into the last open doorway of the corridor. Then, he slowed his pace.

That doorway, you see, led into a room known as The Child's Bedroom: a perfectly-preserved space that gave a real glimpse into the past, thanks to the way its contents – a single wooden bed, a mahogany wardrobe, gauzy drapes and scattering of antique toys – had lain, untouched, for many, many years. All on account of a tragedy that had happened within its walls...

It was a tragedy not everybody knew the details of. There wasn't anything written about it in the Grace Hall guide book. Only a select few – for example, people who'd come to the hall's Halloween party last year, and snagged tickets for a special Ghoulish Guided Tour Lady Tuncaster had organised – knew the full story. And yet, people still seemed to have a sense something awful had happened within the room, because Daniel often heard visitors say it was the one place in the old building that left them a little unnerved.

He could go one better than anyone, though. Because ... because he knew the *victim* of the tragedy. Or, at least, he *had* known her. She'd been the second ghostly figure he'd met that was connected to Grace Hall. Only she, like Wilfred, was supposed to have moved on to the true afterlife. She wasn't supposed to be around any longer.

He hesitated outside the doorway. Could the light he'd been following, really be *her*? He was certainly suspicious that it was. Why else would it have brought him to this part of the hall? And how else to explain the girlish-giggles he'd heard?

Either way, he had to find out what was going on. So he took a deep breath ... then stepped inside the room he hadn't entered for over a year.

The moment Daniel set foot in the old kid's bedroom, something unexpected happened: the door slammed shut behind him.

What the–? He jumped in fright, knowing that, in all the times he'd visited this room in the past, the door had never closed on him, seemingly all by itself!

A trickle of nervous sweat ran down his back. But then his attention was caught by something else. Not the flickering light he'd been following – because one glance around the room showed that seemed to have disappeared.

It had disappeared ... and been replaced with the figure of a little girl.

A little girl who was standing in the middle of the room, on the old scuffed floorboards. She had her back to him but, despite that, Daniel instantly felt a sense of familiarity towards her. The long, dark ringlets, bedecked with violet ribbons, that were tumbling down her back. The dress she was wearing: old-fashioned, white, decorated with frills and ruffles. The little black boots on her feet. Even the way she was peering into a Victorian pram housed in this room, and cooing at the doll he knew lay inside.

All those details – he knew them so well, they made his breath catch in his throat.

This *was* her, wasn't it?! The second spirit he'd met wandering the walls of Grace Hall...

Slowly, as though sensing his eyes on her, the girl turned around. And in that moment Daniel felt an unexpected flash of gratitude for the closed door behind him. Had *she* made that happen? he wondered. To stop visitors interrupting what he now realised was yet *another* unexpected reunion?!

'Cécile?' he exclaimed. 'You've come back?!' Just like Wilfred had, last week? What was going on? he mused, head spinning. Was the unexpected return of the Grace-Hall-ghosts something to do with this time of year, with the special Christmassy energy in the air?!

She smiled prettily up at him. 'Monsieur Daniel! How very good it is to see you again.'

Her adorable French accent hit his ears and made his heart wobble. He was reminded of (once he'd gotten over being freaked out by meeting *another* spook wandering these walls, that was!) how cute he'd always found his little ghost friend. Her petite, heart-shaped face; big, long-lashed dark eyes; dainty smiles. All of that was still just the same as it had been, when he'd known her last year. She hadn't changed at all.

As they looked at each other for a long moment, though, both with delight in their eyes, Daniel realised he was wrong.

Cécile *had* changed. Not in appearance. But ... in some other way. When he'd known her, despite being only a child, she'd always had a bleak, mournful energy swirling around her. An energy that had been puzzling. A little disturbing, even. *Until* Daniel understood the tragedy she'd experienced at Grace Hall, that was. After that, her bleakness had made perfect sense...

Now, though, that sorrowful energy seemed to have disappeared entirely. Instead, the little girl's eyes were soft and contented. Peaceful vibes emanated from her, as though her time in the true afterlife had healed what she'd gone through.

'You're happy,' Daniel uttered. It wasn't even a question. You couldn't mistake the bliss on her face, and he felt a sense of relief and joy at seeing it there. Especially when he thought back to how hard he'd worked, last year, to try and understand *why* this little mite had become trapped within the walls of Grace Hall. When he thought of how hard he'd fought, to free her from the lonely, limbo-land between earth and the true afterlife she'd found herself stuck in.

'*C'est vrai.* I am,' she beamed, in answer. But then her little face turned serious. '*Mais* Daniel – I see that it is different for you. You are *triste*, sorrowful, are you not?'

Daniel felt a jolt of surprise. The last thing he would've expected her to notice was anything about *his* state of mind. She was a child and he was a grown man, after all!

'What? Oh, no. I'm absolutely fine!' he quickly protested, not wanting his little friend to spend even a moment of her time worrying about *him*.

She eyed him carefully, before turning and wandering around the room, her frilly white dress shimmying around her legs as she went. He watched as she looked at all the things she'd left behind, when she'd finally moved on from Grace Hall. Not just Anna, her antique doll which lay in the Victorian pram he'd seen her cooing in at. But a creaky old rocking horse; a chipped tea set; the open wardrobe set against the far wall, which still had clothes hanging inside of it. At first she seemed quite delighted to be reunited with all her old toys and dresses. But, before long, he began to see something shift on her face. Something dark – something of the *old* Cécile – had returned to her eyes, and it made his heart twist with anxiousness.

Sure enough, a beat later, she turned back to him and swallowed. 'I ... I am not sure I want to stay in this place for too long, Daniel.'

Oh, but he understood that. He understood that entirely – given the tragedy she'd endured in this very room. The old sense of protectiveness he used to have towards her made a swift return.

'It's so nice to see you, Cécile. And I'm so happy to know you're doing well. But I agree – you shouldn't stay here too long. You should be with your family.'

She nodded. '*Je suis d'accord. Mais,* I cannot return to the afterlife until I finish the job I came here to do.'

He frowned, not following. What job could a ghost-child possibly have to complete?

'Daniel,' she continued, pointing heavenward. 'There is a man. A man with a – how do you say it – *un grand chapeau*, a large hat – who told me how it was possible to return to visit you.'

A man with a big hat? Daniel instantly thought of Wilfred, and the distinctive top hat he always donned. Was that who she was talking of?!

'And so I came all the way here, to see you. Because no matter what you say, I *know* you are unhappy.' A twinkle of a smile returned to her lips. 'I peek in on you, you see, from where I live now! It is fun to watch you in your shop downstairs. But this year I have seen your smile disappear.' Her face turned sombre again. '*En effet*, look! Your eyes – today they are *especially* sad. *Alors*, this is why I chose this moment to return to you.'

He swallowed and tried again to tell her he was fine – even though he knew that was a lie. She was right. He *was* particularly unhappy today, thanks to his shock at what had happened to Lacey on Saturday night; and to being hit with the realisation he'd been pushing his wife too hard with this fertility battle they were immersed in.

Now he had no baby; *and* a wife who was crumbling around the edges.

His objections only met with Cécile shaking her head, though, so insistently her long ringlets swished around her shoulders.

'Daniel, last year I was all alone. *Solitaire*, lonely. You helped me return to those I love: my mama and papa, my sisters. But before I left you I told you something. I–' she banged her little fist against her chest '–I told you I would never forget your kindness. And so this is why I am here. I want to repay your kindness to me.'

'Cécile! You don't have to do anything for me. I'm just glad I *could* help you–'

'*Non*. Daniel, I insist! *S'il vous plaît* – think of this as my gift to you...'

Just at that, Daniel heard his phone buzz in the back pocket of his jeans. Cécile smiled knowingly at the sound.

'*Bon*.' She clapped her hands together. 'Now you have what you need, I can leave you. But – oh! How I wish I could come with you on your trip.'

His, er, what now? His *trip*? What did she mean by that? Daniel wondered, confused.

She smiled again. '*Ah, oui!* Your trip, to the very special place you must go to! It is a place, you see, that will once again make you happy. But Daniel – promise me, when you're there, that you'll think of me?' she asked, with a tremble in her voice.

'You'll think of how I used to run in the glorious gardens? Of how I used to visit my pretty pony, Louis, in the stables? Of how I used to dance in front of the mirrors in the beautiful *grand salon*?'

Even though he felt confused by her words, Daniel promised he would indeed think of her doing all those things. Not just because he could see that whatever she was talking about clearly meant a lot to her; but because there was no time to do anything else, to ask any more questions about this "special place" she wanted him to visit. Not now her dainty little figure was beginning to turn hazy, in the same way Wilfred's had done last week, before his old friend had once more disappeared to the depths of the afterlife.

His heart quivered, knowing he had only mere moments left in her company. 'Oh, Cécile! It's been so lovely to see you, sweetheart.'

She smiled at him. A beautiful, bright smile. And then, before she faded away completely, she uttered one last thing:

'Goodbye, dearest Daniel. And – *Joyeux Noël.*'

When Cécile left, the old kid's bedroom fell back into silence. For a moment or two Daniel's heart felt heavy. Strange as it might sound, even though she was a child of the spirit world, he still had a special bond with that little girl! And seeing her again had reminded him just how *fatherly* he'd felt towards her last year.

He liked feeling fatherly. It was a responsibility he was more than ready for. Seeing his little friend had reminded him of that all over again.

His eyes flit from the old dolls' house in the corner of the room, to the cracked child's tea set and the little frilly dresses hanging in the wardrobe. Agitation once again surged through him, as he thought of how – over a year on from when Cécile had left Grace Hall – he still had no outlet *for* those wanna-be-a-dad feelings of his.

A long, sad sigh left his lips. But then he thought of the words his little friend had come all this way to say to him.

Words about a "gift"? Of a ... a "special place" he must visit? A place that would once again make him happy?

That sounded lovely; but he had no clue where on earth this special place might be. But then Daniel recalled the way his phone had buzzed in his pocket during Cécile's visit, something that *definitely* seemed to have brought a knowing smile to her face.

Curious, he pulled it out of his pocket.

And what he saw there, on the screen, made him blink in surprise...

THIRTEEN

His phone screen was showing a website.

A website Daniel knew *for certain* he himself hadn't pulled up. Not even accidentally, by clicking on an advert or anything like that – because he hadn't been on Google even once today.

There was a photo at the head of the page. A photo that, once he'd begun looking at it, Daniel found he couldn't drag his eyes away from.

Because the image showed a castle. No – he quickly corrected himself, clocking that the elegant building had a French address. That made it a ... a *château*, didn't it? It was a spectacular-looking building: built in white stone, with graceful, tall windows, and turret after turret that rose into the baby blue sky beyond. It was even surrounded – on each side, and at the back – by a sparkling moat.

It wasn't just the prettiness of the dwelling that caught his attention, though. It was the fact it looked, he frowned, just like a place someone had once described to him. That someone being ... *Cécile*.

Before he could scroll any further through the webpage, he was interrupted by the sound of voices in the corridor outside the bedroom. They gave him a start, and reminded him he was supposed to be back at work by now, in the gift shop, instead of hiding out in Grace Hall's nursery wing!

He quickly opened the still-shut door and hurried back towards the ground floor, giving the visitors on the corridor – who were clearly on their way to viewing The Child's Bedroom – a little wave as he went.

Once he was safely ensconced back behind the shop counter, Daniel pulled out his phone again and retuned to gawping at the photo of the chic château.

It really *did* look like a place Cécile had once told him all about – that place being her family's estate. His little friend, you see, hadn't actually lived at Grace Hall as a kid. As her accent clearly demonstrated, she hailed from across the English Channel. She'd only come to Yorkshire as a visitor ... but had sadly never made it back to her native France.

She'd told Daniel all about the home she'd hailed from, though. Of its turrets and moat and beauty.

Could this really be the same place she'd described? he wondered. Was ... was that why this website had mysteriously appeared on his phone, at the same time as her impromptu return to Grace Hall?

He rattled his brain, then, trying to remember what she'd called her childhood home. A beat later the name came to him: *Château du Bijou*. He recalled thinking, at the time she'd uttered those words, and told him the rough English translation – Jewel Castle – that it sounded like an awfully grand place!

And yet – he hesitated, recalling that he'd actually scoured the internet last year, trying to find any property in France that might bear that very name. The reason being, at the time, he'd begun to struggle with the mystery of why the little girl was lingering on at Grace Hall long after her death; and had hoped finding details of her previous home might throw up some helpful clues as to what had happened to her (because she'd flat refused to speak of the matter, you see).

Despite trawling Google and Google Maps, though, he hadn't found anywhere that remotely matched the stunning home she'd spoken of.

So, despite being a visual match of the home she'd described, could this place *really* be one and the same as Cécile's beloved *Château du Bijou*??

Curious, he found the *About Us* section of the website, and clicked on it. Two smiling faces immediately popped up on the screen.

Hi! the text underneath read. *We're Judy and Larry Miller! And this is our home, the gorgeous Château de Noël.*

Oh. Daniel's shoulders slumped. That settled it, then. *Château de Noël?* This place had entirely the wrong address to be Cécile's French family estate.

But then something, a little further down the page, caught his eye. A name: *de Beaulieu.*

Hang on. That was his little friend's surname! he recalled, with a frown.

OK. Maybe he had to read this page a little more carefully... He went back to the start of the story Judy and Larry had written:

We hail from New York. It's a place we're grateful to, for the wonderful careers it offered us. For its vibrant living, and all the friends we still have there.

But when our son grew up and moved to Los Angeles, we realised we were ready for a change. City life was beginning to wear on us. So we decided to retire, and take a six-week summer vacation to rural France.

Long story short, Côtes d'Armor was so beautiful we never wanted to leave! Inspired by the many stunning old buildings in this part of the world, we went château shopping ... and ended up falling head over heels for the place we now call home!

When we found it, Château du Bijou –

Wow. Hang on! Daniel nearly dropped his phone as he read that part of the text.

Château du Bijou – ancestral home of the de Beaulieu family – had been abandoned and left in a state of disrepair. So sad!

So this *was* Cécile's old home, after all! he breathed.

But we saw the potential to return this gorgeous old building to a wonderful family home. We weren't daunted by the work it needed – we've always enjoyed renovating properties, and we were looking for our next challenge in life!

You might wonder why we changed the property's name. The family crests of the de Beaulieu family will always remain stamped throughout the building. But we wanted to mark the start of this next chapter in the château's existence. So, in honour of the fact the sale was finalised just before Christmas, we settled on a name that has become very special to us: Château de Noël. We think it represents the special, sparkly, snugness of our home just perfectly!

Château de Noël? The Christmas Château? Yes. It *was* a lovely name, Daniel agreed. A name that, especially at this time of year, made him think of crackling open fires; panelled rooms dressed with rich garlands; snowflakes dancing over ornamental gardens.

It was the last part of Judy and Larry's *About Us* section, though, that really caught his attention:

Now, after months of hard work, we're ready to share our beautiful home with the rest of the world. So, if you're in need of a peaceful retreat. If you crave some restorative moments in the serene French countryside, and want to stay in a place that's full of warmth and welcome – then why not treat yourself and reserve one of our bed & breakfast guest rooms? We promise you this: you'll leave feeling like a million dollars!

When he'd finished reading the Millers' story, Daniel set his phone down. He found his head was spinning a little with the unexpected events of the last hour or so.

One thing was for sure. Cécile wanted him to visit the *Château de Noël*, didn't she? Her gift to him was making the place appear on his phone screen, because he'd never have known about its existence otherwise! And she'd said a trip to the property, to the place he now knew to be her old home, would make him "happy again".

He had a feeling she was right, he nodded. He wasn't sure why. But, something about the setting, the beaming faces of the Millers and the prettiness of the château itself, felt like it was calling to him. And then there were the words Judy and Larry had used to describe what a stay to their guesthouse would feel like:

Restorative. Peaceful. You'll leave feeling like a million dollars!

He thought of what a difficult year he and Lacey had been through. Of the unhappiness their infertility was causing in their lives.

Then he mused over how, so far, he hadn't been able to think of a good way to apologise to Lacey for how bossy he'd been lately. Hadn't been able to think of a special way of reminding her of what she meant to him.

Could the *Château de Noël* be the answer?!

One more thing played on his mind… He recalled how it was their wedding anniversary this coming weekend. And of how he still hadn't bought so much as a card for his wife, by way of celebrating the occasion.

Had sweet Cécile just provided the perfect way, not only of bringing a little much-needed peace and "restorative moments" into his and Lacey's lives? But also of playing out some of the advice *Wilfred* had left him with, into the bargain? Daniel wondered eagerly.

Make this a wonderful Christmas – not a wasted one, his old friend had told him.

Maybe he and Lacey couldn't have *quite* the wonderful Christmas they'd dreamt they might, this year, seeing as they wouldn't be celebrating the holiday season with a precious little one of their own.

But having a baby wasn't *everything*. The shock, the fright, his beloved wife keeling over the other night had given him, was a stark reminder, Daniel nodded woefully, that he shouldn't ever overlook the good things he *did* have in his life.

On that note, maybe he could still give Lacey the amazing Christmas she definitely deserved – by kicking off the festive season in style, with a mini-break abroad?

He picked his phone up again and determinedly scrolled through to the Millers' *Book Now!* page...

The château had availability for this coming weekend! That was just what Daniel had been hoping to see. It wasn't going to be cheap to stay there, but Lady Tuncaster had very kindly told all her staff they'd once again be getting a Christmas bonus this year, so he knew he could use that to cover the expense.

The next thing he did was ring Charlotte. He'd quickly decided, you see, that it would be even more special if he made this trip a *secret* escape to the French countryside! He'd tell his wife to expect a flight, and to pack warm clothes, of course. But – he imagined the look of surprise that would come over her face when they rolled up outside the stunning *Château de Noël*, and knew the added intrigue would be worth it!

To make the holiday worthwhile, though, she was going to have to take a couple of days off from work. Thankfully, after he'd filled Charlotte in on his plans – *and* asked her to keep quiet about them! – she assured him she and Cooper could cover Lacey's schedule.

'Honestly, honey, I've been a little worried about her since she clean collapsed on us at the F-Group party. I feel awful I didn't realise she'd been having dizzy spells before then. This is probably just what she needs – a break to re-charge her batteries, right? So don't worry – I'll take care of everything this end. You just get that gorgeous-sounding château booked!'

Perfect! Daniel smiled and thanked her for being so kind. Then he wished her and Cooper an amazing trip to Boston – he was certain *they* were going to have a brilliant Christmas, with such a fab holiday in the works – before ringing off.

Right. There was just one more thing, he nodded, that he had to accomplish before he could officially make his booking to go and stay at Cécile's old home: he had to find out if Neville would grant *him* some leave for the trip...

It was a thought that suddenly made him nervous. Was he being *too* optimistic, that he could pull off this whole romantic-trip-to-the-*Côtes-d'Armor* plan, at such short notice?

Because the leave he was going to need to be granted, Daniel knew, would include a Saturday shift.

And Saturdays – especially at Christmas time – were the busiest day of the week at Grace Hall...

With that thought in mind, as soon as his afternoon tea break rolled around Daniel hurried across the gravel drive to the barn conversion where Neville's office was based.

'Daniel! Come in. How are you this fine afternoon?'

His boss was his usual welcoming self when he tapped gently on the door of his empty-coffee-cup-and-paper-strewn room. Despite that, Daniel still felt apprehensive as he stepped inside.

'I'm good, thanks. That is, well ... er ...' He scratched his head, suddenly unsure how to ask his boss for the time off he needed. Or, rather, how to ask – in a way that might guarantee the response he wanted.

Neville stopped thumbing through a stack of files and looked across his desk with a frown. 'Oh, dear. Is everything quite alright? You look worried.'

'I ... well, I was just wondering? If I could ask a favour?' Daniel finally admitted. And then, once he started talking, the words simply tumbled out of him. More words than he'd even meant to say.

His concerns over Lacey after her fainting spell the other night. His idea (well of course, it was really *Cécile's* idea, but he couldn't let that on to his boss!) of treating her to a mini-holiday to France. Of how he'd love to make it happen this coming weekend, since it was their second wedding anniversary and – he hung his head as he admitted this part – his mind had been so full of other things lately, he'd not planned anything else to celebrate the occasion...

On and on he went, until Neville pushed back his chair and stood up. He walked round to where Daniel was standing ... and pressed a hand to his shoulder.

A hand that was so steady and warm, it made Daniel instantly stop waffling.

'It's fine,' Neville said gently.

Daniel blinked, a little confused by his boss's response – because he hadn't even got to the part of asking for any days off yet!

'You're going to ask, I presume,' Neville continued, 'if you can take some leave? For this break? Make a long weekend of it? Well, the answer is ... yes. Of course you can.'

'Oh, wow, really? I'm sorry it's such short notice–'

Neville squeezed his shoulder.

'Don't be sorry. Daniel, since you joined us here at Grace Hall, you've been a marvellous employee. Simply marvellous! Hard working and dedicated. Lady Tuncaster and I appreciate all your efforts.

'But I'm also,' he hesitated, his face creasing in sympathy, *'aware,* shall we say, what a difficult year you and Lacey have had. I'm sorry for your troubles, I really am. But for all those reasons, quite frankly I'll man the gift shop myself, if that's what it takes for you and Lacey to go on this trip! You deserve a chance to have a little time for yourselves and enjoy your anniversary.'

He nodded vehemently, showing how much he meant those words. And Daniel was left feeling not just grateful ... but ashamed.

Neville – ever since they'd first met, he'd always been this way towards him, he realised. Kind. The man was kind to his core. And it made him feel awful, suddenly, for the sniffy way he'd taken the news that his boss would be joining them at his mum's house on Christmas Day.

He had to get over himself, Daniel nodded. *Of course* – even all these years later – it was going to be strange to see his mum with another guy. To have another man spending time, in the home they'd once shared with his dad.

But Neville was his mum's second chance at love and she couldn't have found herself a better man. She really couldn't. She was in the best of hands.

It was time he quit being selfish and supported both of them in their new life together, Daniel told himself firmly.

Besides, deep down, he knew that was what his dad would want.

He reached up and touched Neville's hand, which was still pressed to his shoulder.

'Thank you. Thank you so much! And when we're back from our trip, we're looking forward to spending Christmas with you and my mum. It's going to be a lovely day,' Daniel told him.

It was only a couple of sentences; but they were a start in putting things right. And he was immediately rewarded by seeing Neville's cheeks turn pink in pleasure.

'Oh. Th ... thank you for saying that, Daniel. Thank you indeed. It *will* be a lovely day. A wonderful day! And I'm very grateful, you know. To you and your mum – and Lacey, of course – for including me in your plans.' His voice turned a little quiet as he added, 'It means the world to have people to celebrate the day with, this year.'

That last remark made Daniel feel another wash of shame. To think he'd known, too, that his boss – thanks to having no family of his own – had nobody else to share the holiday with! That knowledge should've made him way more compassionate and welcoming right from the start.

He bit his lip and hoped he'd never be so selfish again. And then he thought of all the other lonely souls out there. Other people who, for whatever reason, would find themselves with nobody to celebrate Christmas Day with. Who would sit in their homes on December 25th, feeling forgotten as the world partied on around them.

Those with no family, like Neville. Those who were estranged from their families. Those with toxic relations, who deliberately left them out of plans. People who'd moved away from familiar neighbourhoods, for work. Those suffering with their mental health. The elderly. The shy. The friendless. The vulnerable.

Oh! Daniel's heart wobbled and he sent out a silent wish, right there and then, that everyone who was in a position to, would find a way to include at least one lonely person in their plans this Christmas period. Because he imagined that even the smallest act of kindness could make a huge difference to someone's life at this time of year. To making them feel included. To making them feel *human* ... instead of left out in the cold.

An invite to enjoy a mince pie and a cuppa in your home. A Christmas Eve hot chocolate at a local café. An hour or two spent watching some seasonal TV with an elderly neighbour. There were countless ways to be kind at this time of year.

And as for him? *His* act of kindness, Daniel decided firmly, would be to ensure he did everything he could to make Neville feel welcome in his family this festive season.

FOURTEEN

As people bustled past her, wheeling suitcases, chattering, peering at boarding passes, Lacey felt like she was in a dream.

How, she wondered again, could she currently be standing in an airport? In France? About to head off in a hire car to goodness-knew-where ... when she'd fully expected, instead, to be at work today, in the centre of drizzly York?!

She shook her head, really quite dazed by the unforeseen events that had gone on in her life this past week...

Obviously, to start with, the F-Group Christmas party hadn't panned out how she'd thought it would. Of course, most of the night had been amazing and great fun. But it had been a real shock to pass out, then find herself in the care of those lovely paramedics, Chaaya and Toby. But after her blood sugar had finally returned to safe levels, thanks to the great big plate of food everyone had insisted she eat from the buffet, she and Daniel had decided to cut the night short and head home.

He'd been quiet much of the drive back, Lacey remembered. In fact, he'd looked whiter than *she* did, by the time they made it back to the cottage. That had been her fault, of course, for giving him a fright.

Her fault, too, no doubt, for putting him in the stressful situation of having to watch as she *very definitely* broke their clean eating plan of late, with handfuls of crisps and that huge chunk of decadent chocolate fudge cake...

Anyway. She'd been feeling guilty all week for how the night had ended. And confused, too. Despite, you see, the fact her worried mum had been dropping round to the cottage these past days, with all sorts of carb-heavy food designed to "build her up" – vegetable lasagne and garlic bread and shepherd's pie – she still wanted to show Daniel she was 100% on board with doing anything he thought could improve their chances of conceiving. Still wanted him to know that showing up for him, in a way she hadn't last year, was her absolute priority in life.

But it was also obvious, Lacey knew, that Chaaya had made some valid points: running around with a low blood sugar, day after day, *wasn't* healthy; she needed to be strong, to conceive; and her dizzy spells and collapse were a sign she wasn't taking care of herself as well as she'd *thought* she was, by following her husband's healthy-lifestyle-plan to the letter.

Clearly, she and Daniel needed to have a talk about those points. But thanks to this surprise trip he'd booked, there hadn't ended up being time to sit down and discuss *anything*, so far this week!

Lacey looked bemusedly around the airport she was standing in once more. Listened as an announcement – one she couldn't understand a word of, given it was spoken in rapid French! – blasted out over the tannoy system. And then she clocked Daniel, squeezing through the crowds near the rental car kiosks. He was heading back towards her with a smile and a set of car keys in his hand, a sight that made her heart flutter.

Honestly. She'd believed, hadn't she? That, given how distracted and angst-y and worried her husband had been these past months – thanks to their not falling pregnant – that he wasn't interested in making any fuss around their anniversary this year. Something she could understand – even if part of her had also, deep down, been a little worried of how he was *really* feeling, towards a marriage that wasn't providing him with the child he wanted so badly.

So when he'd told her, on Monday night, that he was actually whisking her off on a secret trip to celebrate the occasion, she ... well, she'd almost keeled over again, only this time from surprise!

He hadn't given away many details, which gave the whole thing an even more romantic and mysterious vibe. He'd simply said he'd arranged for her to have Friday and Monday off work, so they could make a long weekend of it (thank you, Charlotte!); that the trip would involve a short plane ride; and that her mum and Maz were going to look after Emme while they were away.

Three days of frantically getting organised had followed ... and now, before she'd barely blinked, it was Friday afternoon, and here they were, at Rennes Bretagne airport.

As they headed for the hire car parking lot, Lacey realised Daniel was looking at her in a way he hadn't done in a long time.

She took in the softness in his eyes, the little smile on his lips, the way he nudged her gently with his elbow as they exited the sliding doors of the airport and stepped into the bitterly-cold-but-blue-sky-day outside.

'Are you looking forward to finding out where we're going?' he asked.

She smiled eagerly, keen to show him how much she appreciated this gesture he was making. 'Absolutely! This is so exciting.'

He nodded ... but his eyes still lingered on her face, this time in a way that made a little nervousness ripple through her. Truth was, lovely as her husband had been this week, especially with his secret-anniversary-plans, she still wasn't quite sure how to feel around him right now. Or what was going on in his mind.

Lacey reflected, again, on the moments that'd followed her coming round from her faint at the F-Group party. Of the panic she'd felt over how Daniel might react to the situation: *especially* to the evidence she clearly hadn't been looking after herself in the way he'd kept telling her to.

I'm sorry. I can't believe I fainted like that! I ... I'll look after myself better in future. I promise I will. Don't be mad with me.

If she was honest, she was still waiting for him to get upset with her. After all, his only aim right now was for them to get pregnant, so it couldn't have been easy for him to see her lying out on the floor like that.

She should've contacted a doctor earlier about her dizzy spells. She shouldn't have let things escalate to a situation where she'd needed the help of *paramedics*! Then again, she'd only gotten dizzy – because she hadn't been eating enough. And she'd only not been eating enough ... because she'd been trying to keep Daniel happy by following his healthy living plan!

Yup. They *definitely* needed to talk, she thought again. Because one thing had certainly become obvious at the weekend – things couldn't go on like this.

They found their rental car – a little blue hatchback – then headed out of the airport. Daniel let on that they'd be travelling towards the northwest of the country. At first, the roads were busy, and he was a little jittery as his brain adapted to driving on a different side of the road to back home in the UK! Eventually, though, as they headed away from the city of Rennes, the roads grew quieter, and it started to really feel like they were headed off on an adventure. Especially when, 'Côtes d'Armor. That's where we're going to be staying,' Daniel eventually told her.

Oh. That sounded lovely, Lacey smiled. Very French indeed!

After an hour or so, they began to swing away from the main roads and moved, instead, into terrain that turned more rural. Towns turned into cute villages. The road they were travelling along grew narrow. Green field after green field rolled out before them.

But then things turned a little more complicated. The deeper they drove into the charming countryside, the more Daniel began to frown at his mapping system. As the sun began to dip in the sky, he made a few wrong turns, travelling down bumpy lanes that led to nowhere – well, that led to him uttering a few choice swear words, then turning back in the direction they'd just come from, that was!

Eventually, though, one of the lanes they turned into seemed to be exactly the place Daniel was looking for. Lacey knew it was, because his face brightened with relief as they drove through a set of old iron gates with a sign pinned to them: *Le Château de Noël.*

Le Château de Noël? She didn't know *much* French; but she did know enough to realise that translated as meaning The Christmas Château. But – what a pretty name! she was about to exclaim.

She didn't, though. The reason being, at the end of the tree-lined, rutted driveway they were rattling along, something else captured her attention...

Lacey stared out through the windscreen. Just like at the airport earlier, she once again felt like she was in a dream.

Because there, revealing itself at the far end of the drive, was the most breathtakingly beautiful building she'd ever seen in her life.

It rose up from the ground. A gracious white-stoned château, with a steep grey roof and turret after turret, that spiralled skyward. The windows were arched and slender, and framed with shutters painted in an exquisite shade of china blue. A moat sparkled around the sides of the property, and gorgeous topiary trees in slate planters were set on either side of the double, ivory-coloured entrance doors.

'This can't be where we're staying.' Lacey, open-mouthed, looked at her husband. He grinned back at her from the driver's seat – amused, no doubt, by the shocked expression she knew she was rocking.

'It is!' he laughed. 'It *is* where we're staying. But I know how you feel – I was blown away too, when I saw the photos of this place on the website.'

'It looks like a fairy-tale castle or something. Daniel – this is incredible!'

She nearly had to pinch herself, she was so surprised by the location she found herself in. When she'd realised they were coming to France, Lacey nodded, she'd thought perhaps they would be staying in a cute gîte or at a guesthouse in a little market town, something like that. Not a place that looked fit for a queen to visit! In fact, she suddenly felt embarrassed as she thought of the monogrammed towels *she'd* bought Daniel as her anniversary present – how lame, in comparison to this treat he'd arranged for her! She was going to have to up her game!

They parked up beside some other vehicles. As she got out of the car Lacey gazed again at the building, this time noticing the way the setting sun was illuminating the white stone, giving off vibes of warmth and welcome. She noticed, too, the pretty gardens set off to either side of the moat. They were almost as gorgeous as the home they flanked, with their sections of evergreen hedging; flowerbeds bursting with pink winter camellias; honeysuckle, that floated up old sections of wall; and meandering gravel walkways, that looked so inviting she found herself itching to explore.

Wow. Just – *wow*, she thought again.

Just then a lady – who looked to be in her early sixties, judging by her gently-lined skin and steel-grey hair – appeared by the front door. She was dressed in jeans and a burgundy, cowl neck sweater. She was also wearing a pair of huge glasses; thick, gold hoop earrings; and had a smile on her face, so bright it put Lacey instantly at ease.

'Hey guys! I'm Judy, the owner here at the château. You must be the Hargreaves. Welcome! Did you find us OK?'

Daniel admitted to getting a little lost on the way, to which Judy laughed.

'You're not alone there, sugar! Most people get confused en-route. *We* ended up slap, bang in the middle of a field, first time we visited the place. The farmer still tells us off for bouncing over his crops in our Range Rover!'

She winked at them both, then called back into the house. 'Hey, Larry – our new guests are here! Come say hi.'

A moment later a bald-headed bloke, who had a thick dark beard and was dressed in a green checked flannel shirt, popped up next to her.

'Hey! Hello!' He pointed to himself. 'Larry, Judy's husband. Welcome to our home! Daniel and Lacey, isn't it? I remember from your booking. Let's get you guys settled in.'

As Daniel and Larry extracted the luggage from the boot of the car, Judy threaded her arm through Lacey's and showed her into the château's interior.

'It's getting cold, out,' Judy noted. 'But don't worry —we've got a huge fire going in the salon, to keep you warm!'

Lacey smiled gratefully. That sounded lovely. Because, with the sun now setting, the nip in the air outside was growing stronger.

Turned out they didn't even make it to the salon, though, before she found herself coming to a stop and gawping at her surroundings once more...

'Oh. This is beautiful!' The moment she stepped over the threshold, Lacey found herself standing in an impressive, double-height hallway. It had distressed, dark wood floorboards; sets of double doors leading off to different rooms; and ornate brass sconces to light the warm, creamy-mushroom-coloured walls. Also, off to one side, there was a curving staircase leading up to the first floor, which boasted a gorgeous, swirling, wrought-iron balustrade.

'Thank you sugar.' Judy pressed a hand to her chest. 'We are pleased with how it's all turned out!'

'And you did all this yourself, didn't you?' Daniel, coming in behind them with his rucksack in hand, said he'd read the Millers' story on their website.

Lacey's eyes widened as she heard of the derelict state the château had been in, when Judy and Larry were first shown the place by a local *agent immobilier*.

'It's been a hell of a lot of work,' Larry said, a touch ruefully. 'But we have had help from some awesome contractors, along the way.'

'That's true,' Judy nodded. 'And, besides, we could never have gone back to New York and forgotten about this place, like some of our friends warned us we should do. Not after we'd set eyes on her and fallen clean in love!

'Yeah, she's certainly been our passion project. We brought the old girl back to life. And now we feel like we belong here. But we want to share our home's beautiful energy with others, too – because she is *fabulous*!'

Everyone laughed in agreement. As Judy and Larry smiled at each other, Lacey thought of how – even after only being in their company for five minutes – she could tell what an amazing couple the pair were. Full of drive and warmth and kindness. And then Larry took their bags upstairs, while Judy prepared to show them into the salon.

'Let's get you kids a warm drink before we show you to your room. Now, the salon can be used by you anytime you like, during your stay. We want you to feel right at home. Speaking of which...' Before they left the entrance hall, their hostess gestured at the many doorways they were surrounded by.

'Have a wander around the château, too. We leave the doors open to rooms you can take a peek at. I know people are always curious to see more of the property than just their *chambre*!'

Aw, how kind and welcoming was that?! Lacey smiled. And then – if she'd thought the hallway was impressive – she realised she was in for an even greater treat as they followed Judy into the guest lounge, situated at the front of the property.

The salon looked like something out of a posh interiors magazine. That was her first thought, the moment she stepped through the arched double doors and set eyes on the room that had to be the gem of the old building.

Plush, cream velvet sofas were arranged around an antique walnut coffee table. Umpteen tall, slender windows, reaching from floor to ceiling, lined the room, and Lacey could only imagine how much light would spill through them in the summer months, illuminating the panelled, soft taupe walls inside. Each window frame was dressed with rich, dark blue silk curtains, that shimmered and pooled decadently on the dark wooden floor. As Judy had promised, there was also a fire crackling in the room's pale marble fireplace, which warmed the space beautifully. And, in keeping with the château's pretty name, a huge fir Christmas tree, which was giving off a fresh, menthol-y scent, stood elegantly in one corner. It was dressed with gold and white baubles, which matched perfectly with both the gold tassels holding back the silk curtains; *and* the gold-tipped holly garland strung across the mantel shelf.

'Wow. I adore this room!' Lacey gushed. Truly, what *was* this magical place Daniel had brought her to?!

Judy laughed in delight, at her on-going enthusiastic reaction to her home. But Daniel – he didn't say anything. Instead, he seemed drawn to the fireplace. He stared at the over-mantel, which was filled mostly with a huge, old, dappled mirror; but which also had an intricate carving set into the base. It was the carving that particularly seemed to have caught his attention. To the point that a strange look – a look that was almost wistful – slid over his face, as he ran his fingers slowly along the etching.

'Ah. You've found the family crest. Beautiful, isn't it?' Judy sighed. 'This place was built for the *de–*'

'For the *de Beaulieu* family,' Daniel nodded, almost dazedly. Then he turned round and blinked. 'Sorry. I didn't mean to interrupt you there. I, er ... I just,' he waved his hands around, 'remember reading about the family. On your, um, website.'

'That's OK, sugar! It's just such a shame the family line eventually died out. That's why this place fell to wrack and ruin.'

'Well.' He looked around, and another strangely reflective look filled his face. 'You've done an incredible job bringing it back to its former glory. I ... I'm sure the original family would be so grateful, for all your hard work,' he added quietly.

Judy looked touched by his words. Then she went off to fix them some coffee – Lacey tried to pull some camomile teabags out of her handbag and say she'd have a herbal tea instead; but Daniel surreptitiously shook his head and made her put them away.

'We're on holiday. A cup of coffee here or there isn't going to do you any harm,' he nodded.

Oh. That was a very unexpected thing for him to say. Because he'd been really quite ferociously determined – after one of his how-to-improve-our-fertility reading sessions on Google – that they should, for now, remove every trace of caffeine from their diet. (In contrast, Lacey had read that drinking caffeine in moderation was perfectly fine, maybe even beneficial, for fertility; something she'd tactfully decided not to mention all these months, for fear of rocking the boat.)

Maybe, she considered, he was simply being polite in front of the Millers? Just in case, when Judy brought a cafetière and some vintage cups through to the salon a short time later, she made sure to take only a few sips of the coffee their hostess poured for them. That was despite the fact it was so rich and creamy – such a perfect drink to enjoy in the beautiful, decadent surroundings she found herself in – that Lacey could have easily enjoyed a whole mug!

And then it was time to be shown upstairs by Larry, to a room that certainly lived up to the standard of décor they'd already witnessed downstairs...

The bedroom they'd be staying in was situated on the east side of the building, and they had to walk along a soft-cream-carpeted hallway – lined with gilt-framed portraits of elegant-looking ladies from long ago – to reach it. When Larry threw open the door, Lacey saw the space behind was another masterpiece in chic French design!

A large antique bedframe, with an upholstered, off-white high headboard, sat against one wall. It was dressed with beautifully soft bed linen and white silk cushions. Shimmering, smoky-coloured damask curtains framed the tall windows. The walls were panelled and painted in ivory; and an eye-catching, crystal-and-iron pendant hung from the high ceiling. There was also a seating area, complete with plump, white wing chairs and a low slung, pale grey coffee table; and a gorgeous, Christmas-themed vase of flowers – deep red roses, winterberries and pine needles – arranged on a side dresser. Finally, there was an en-suite bathroom, modern and luxurious, with brushed nickel taps; double sinks; a beautiful rainfall shower head; and posh, opaque-bottled toiletries.

Once again, Lacey found herself wide-eyed with admiration. 'How stunning!' she breathed, as she wandered around the space she could hardly believe she was going to have the privilege of sleeping in for the next three nights. Daniel was full of compliments, too, and Larry smiled.

'Well, great to hear you love the place! Now, what are you kids planning to do for dinner? We can whip something up for you in the kitchen – there's a little menu on your dresser over there. Or, if you'd prefer to eat out, the nearest town – Tierné – is about a ten minute drive away. There're a couple of restaurants, but we'd definitely recommend the local crêperie, *Pour L'Amour des Crêpes*. You can have a savoury pancake for your main, then a sweet one for dessert. *Parfait*, am I right?!' he laughed.

Daniel and Lacey looked at each other. 'A crêperie? That *does* sound perfect!' Daniel grinned. Lacey smiled in agreement.

Larry shot them a thumbs up, said to shout if they needed anything – "anything at all" – then left them in peace.

When he'd gone, Lacey couldn't help but talk about the room again.

'Daniel! I'm so grateful you brought me here. What a place! I've never stayed in a guesthouse as pretty as this before.' She wandered around again, running her fingers over the silky curtains and bed linen; peeked out of the window – they had a view of the moat and gardens from this side, although it was hard to see much now it had gone dark outside; then went to the bathroom to try out some of the organic rose hand cream she'd spotted in there.

When she came back, she found Daniel sitting on the edge of the bed. He looked at her and smiled, softly.

'I'm so glad you love the château. Y … you deserve this break. You really do.'

His smile disappeared, to be replaced with a heavy sigh. It was a sound that made Lacey snap out of the dreamy state she'd fallen into.

Why was he sighing? What was wrong? And why had his smile vanished?

Just the same as when they'd been walking out of the airport earlier, Lacey was suddenly reminded that, despite the beautiful setting they now found themselves in, there were still things lurking between her and her husband they hadn't had a chance to talk about yet. Like how he was feeling towards her, since her collapse last weekend. Like her worries that he – despite this amazing break he'd organised for their anniversary – might be secretly annoyed at witnessing for himself that she clearly hadn't been taking care of herself as well as he wanted her to. And what that might mean for their chances of falling pregnant this month...

On that note, 'Look at this area,' she suddenly blurted, pointing to the generous space, covered with a pearly, chenille rug, that lay between the bed and the window. 'It's perfect for doing my yoga! I packed some leggings, so I can keep up my practice while we're here. How about I take ten minutes to do some stretches before we head out for dinner?'

Her voice was breathy, rushed. But she couldn't help herself. She wanted to make Daniel at ease again, like he'd been five minutes ago. And the only thing that seemed guaranteed to make him relax this year, was showing that she was steadfast in following all his healthy-lifestyle instructions!

He didn't react how she'd expected him to, though...

'Oh my God. Lacey!' he exclaimed, in a voice so woeful she found herself staring at him. 'You don't need to do *yoga* right now! Like I said downstairs – we're on holiday.'

Lacey hesitated. She scratched her head in confusion. Hm. Firstly, her caffeine-hating husband tells her it's fine for her to have a cup of coffee; and now he was saying she could skip the daily yoga practice he'd been so adamant for months, now, could help them have a baby?? She was sure people would think she was mad for finding such silly little issues perplexing. But the way Daniel had been, this year? How insistent he'd been that *every single little choice* they made, could determine whether or not they finally got to have a child of their own? That kind of intense drive didn't just disappear overnight. It just didn't.

Her bewilderment must have shown on her face, because his eyes turned sad.

'Look what I've done. I've made you *nervous* of me. What kind of a husband have I turned into?!'

He hung his head. Lacey rushed over to the bed and sat next to him.

'What? No! I'm not *nervous* of you!' Her voice turned awfully high-pitched as she blurted that last remark, which was enough for both of them to see that she was lying.

'You are,' Daniel nodded sagely. 'The way you look at me these days, like you're walking on eggshells all the time? It's awful to see. I hate what I've done to you. To us!'

Lacey swallowed. Given what he was saying, maybe it was time to stop pretending. Because she *was* anxious around him these days, wasn't she? Especially so after her fainting episode at the F-Group party! But it wasn't *him*, as a person, she was feeling tentative towards. She was simply nervous of making the agitated mood he always seemed to be sporting, any worse.

She was just about to reach for his hand and tell him all of that ...when her tummy rumbled. And she meant – it *really* rumbled, loudly, out into the room. Which probably wasn't surprising: they'd only had a sandwich on the plane, and a small snack of a peanut-oat bar and some dried fruit in the car on the way here. But it *was* bad timing ... because it rudely interrupted the moment between them.

Daniel, looking a little panicked, immediately jumped off the bed.

'You're hungry? Then we need to eat.'

'But ... can't we talk, first?'

He shook his head. 'No way. I can't have your blood sugar dropping again! Your mum'd kill me! Not to mention those paramedics said we need to get you strong again. So let's get freshened up and head out. ASAP.'

*

Even on the dark roads surrounding the château, they managed to find their way to Tierné ... without taking any wrong turns this time!

Lit up by old streetlamps, the town's shuttered buildings looked quaint and appealing. And it was easy to find the crêperie Larry had spoken of – because there were only a couple of store fronts that still had lights on inside.

Daniel parked up at the side of the road. When they got out of the car they realised it had turned so cold, they could see their breath in the frosty air. So they hurried towards the restaurant whose swirly-lettered frontage declared it to be *Pour L'Amour des Crêpes*, keen for both some good food *and* to be back in the warmth!

Inside, the crêperie was decorated with red-checked tablecloths and wicker-backed chairs. A single crimson carnation, plus a flickering tea light, was set on each table. The lighting was low, and there were reams of red tinsel woven around the beams on the ceiling. The place seemed popular, given that many of the tables were filled with chattering, laughing diners, all speaking in French, who had big glasses of red wine and enticing plates of stuffed pancakes set out before them.

A polite server – "*Bonsoir Monsieur, Madame*" – showed them to a table for two; then, with the help of a translation app on their phones, they began to decipher the menu.

'I think I'll just have a savoury pancake – a *galette*, I think that's called? Filled with ratatouille.' Lacey decided. 'I bet the veggies they use are from local farms. They'll probably taste amazing.'

She expected Daniel would be happy with that choice. Ratatouille, on a savoury crêpe, was a pretty healthy option, right?

Instead of nodding in agreement, though, she was surprised to see her husband set down his menu and shake his head. Really quite adamantly.

'No. Lacey – no!'

No?!

'This is our anniversary weekend. We're celebrating. So you *can't* just have a boring savoury galette. I mean, I'm sure it will taste amazing. But you most definitely have to have a sweet crêpe for dessert, too! Don't they sound *so* nice?! I *know* they're something you'd love.'

He was right there. Lacey had already snuck a peek at the *Sweet* section of the menu, and felt her mouth water at the decadent options listed: you could have a crêpe topped with cream, ice cream, maple syrup, strawberries, walnuts, sticky chocolate sauce... The list went on.

'But, Daniel – the sugar?'

Given the way they'd been living these past months, it was surely an obvious question for her to ask. But it was met with her husband shaking his head once again and looking ... well, really quite ashamed. Which made Lacey lift her eyebrows in surprise.

'The sugar? Oh, man.' His face crumpled. 'I can't believe things have come to this. That you're asking permission from me for what you can eat at a flipping restaurant.'

He leant across the table and looked earnestly at her. 'Look, Lacey. I've been doing a lot of thinking this week. And I owe you an apology. I've been such a ... a *blockhead* lately!'

A *what*? A *blockhead*? That was a weirdly old-fashioned-sounding insult for her husband to call himself, Lacey frowned.

'I didn't see it at first. But after you blacked out last weekend? Let's just say – you gave me a shock.'

'I'm so sorry, I didn't mean to–'

'No, no. It was a shock I think I needed. If that's not too awful a thing to say. Besides, *I'm* the one who's sorry...'

He took a deep breath then went on to explain how – far from blaming *her* for fainting, the way she was worried he would – he felt the whole thing was his fault. What the paramedics had said, about her overdoing things? Seeing what the end result had been on her body? It made him realise he'd been driving her too hard this year. That he'd become too obsessive, when it came to their attempts to conceive.

'It's ironic, really. I was so desperate for us to be as healthy as possible because, honestly, I just believed that was the way for us to finally fall pregnant. But all I've actually been doing is making our lives more stressful and *less* healthy!' He pressed his hands to his flushed-pink-with-shame cheeks.

'Lace, I'm sorry. You've been such a sweetheart, going along with everything I asked of you. When, really, you should've been telling me not to be so annoying and bossy!'

'Oh, Daniel. I couldn't have done that,' she rued. It was her turn to hang her head. 'Not ... not when I *owe you*. Owe you big time!'

He hesitated, looked a little confused. 'Um. I'm not following. What do you mean by *that*?'

It was her turn to talk. To explain how *she'd* been feeling, of late. Of the guilt she'd been carrying around, ever since grasping a baby wasn't going to come easy for them.

'I probably do look weak, or like a pushover or something,' she acknowledged. 'I did whatever you wanted without question. But ... Daniel, you were so understanding of me last year! So patient, too, when I needed to work through all my issues around being a mum.

'So,' she shrugged, 'this year it's been *my* turn to support you. I wanted you to see that I'm all in when it comes to us having a baby, in a way I wasn't, last year. Plus, I feel awful. That all those months I spent worrying about whether I could be a mother or not, could've been put to better use. We could've started trying sooner, for a little one. That time might have made a difference to where we are now. Honestly.' She swallowed, felt a tightness in her tummy. 'That thought just haunts me.'

'Well it shouldn't.' Daniel didn't even hesitate in his reassurance, which was something that made Lacey's heart swell with love. 'You were going through something last year. You *needed* that time. And now it means you're ready to be an awesome mum! I just really hope a baby *does* happen for us. But it won't, if I keep pushing you to the point your body starts crumbling.'

He looked all upset again. A silence fell between them. But only for a moment, because Lacey reached across the table for her husband's hand, and squeezed it, softly.

'I really hope it happens for us, too,' she said gently. 'In the meantime–' she thought of the lovely Chaaya's advice, of how the paramedic had sensibly pointed out Lacey needed to *support* her body, rather than overdo things '– maybe we need to re-group. Try and be a bit more balanced, going forward.

'Because I think we have to face the fact it could be a long road to getting what we want. And if … if we end up needing IVF, that could be tough. We need to get strong – and stay strong. Steady, too. Don't you think?'

Daniel nodded quickly, words of agreement tumbling out of his mouth. 'Definitely. *Definitely*. That makes so much sense. I only wish I'd been steadier, earlier. I feel like I've put an extra load on your shoulders that you really didn't need.'

Lacey told him it was OK. That she understood – that *lots* of people would understand – how crazy it could make you, not being able to have a child that you craved, wanted, *needed* in your life, so badly.

'I feel off-centre and upset, half the time. I think probably any couple going through infertility is allowed to feel – act, even – *a bit* deranged.'

'True,' Daniel said ruefully. 'You know what, though?' He leant forward again, and a pensive look crossed his face. 'You know I said I've done a lot of thinking this week? Well, I think I've also worked something out about myself, that I didn't understand before. I realise now what's making me *so* desperate to become a dad. It's not just the obvious – that we want to have a family of our own. It's something more. It's … well, it's Neville.'

Lacey blinked. Er, what now? Neville? But … what could her husband's boss possibly have to do with their baby-making plans?!

She must have looked quite surprised indeed by that name-drop, because Daniel threw out a little laugh.

'Sorry. I just realised how strange that must sound. All I'm trying to say, is…'

He went on to elaborate. That having Neville come into his mum's life, that seeing the guy in his childhood home on a regular basis, had made him think much more than usual about his late dad, this year.

'It's made me wonder more about what life *might* have been like, if he hadn't gotten sick. All that time we lost out on – it's so sad. I mean, I was only nine when he died. At least I can remember him, but we didn't get much time together.

'And I think part of me has latched on to the idea that, if *I* become a father, maybe it's a way of filling that void. Maybe, through my own child, I can kinda make up for some of the things I missed out on with *my* dad. I dunno.' He blushed and shuffled awkwardly in his chair, which made Lacey feel a rush of sympathy. 'Does that sound weird?'

'Oh, sweetheart, of course it doesn't. Losing your dad so young – it's a big trauma. So what you've just said makes perfect sense. It makes *me* understand you a little better, too.'

She squeezed his hand supportively, and he shot her a lopsided smile.

'Thanks Lace. I didn't think there would be enough going on in *my* head for any sort of psychoanalysis or whatever, but there you go!'

She giggled.

'I don't want to be desperate any more, though. Determined, yes. But not desperate. It's not good for anyone. So–' he lifted the glass of water the waiter had brought along with their menus '–I know it's not much to toast with. And I know my toast isn't going to sound very exciting. But here's to what you said. To steadiness. To balance, going forward.'

'And to hope,' Lacey added, raising her own glass.

'Yes. *Definitely* to hope.'

They chinked their glasses, then looked lovingly at one another across the table. Lacey realised she suddenly felt loads lighter after their *tête à tête*, as though someone had lifted a rucksack weighed down with rocks off her shoulders.

'So – balance, hey? Does that mean I can quit drinking spirulina smoothies every day?' she smiled wryly.

Daniel laughed and pressed a hand to his forehead. 'Oh God. Yup. That's something else I need to apologise to you for – making you drink flipping algae juice. Honestly, Lace. I think I lost the plot for a while there.'

'I still loved you. I'll always love you.'

His face softened at her words. And then he looked across the table, so adoringly, so devotedly, that Lacey felt her heart melt like the wax in the flickering tea light before them.

'I love you too, my amazing wife. And no matter what happens in the future, that's something that'll *never* change...'

FIFTEEN

When Lacey woke the next morning, in their beautiful château bedroom, with Daniel dozing softly next to her, she realised she felt more contented than she had in ages. Obviously she was still sad, still disappointed, that there was no chance of her becoming a mother in time for this Christmas. But ... she turned her head to her husband. Took in his tousled dark hair, his handsome face, his steady presence, and felt a rush of love.

She might not have *everything* she wanted in life; but she had so much to be thankful for – her gorgeous husband; her family; her job; even this unexpected weekend break in such a stunning place. And she was determined, today – in the spirit of balance, that they'd agreed on last night – to let that gratitude fill her heart for once, instead of sorrow.

Next to her, Daniel's eyelids flickered open.

'Hey you.' The first thing he did was reach for her, and pull her into his arms. 'Happy anniversary,' he murmured, kissing her neck.

'Happy anniversary!' Lacey smiled back. Because that was yet another thing she had to be grateful for, wasn't it? Today officially marked that she and Daniel had been married for a whole two years!

She snuggled close to her love, enjoying the feel of his warm body next to hers. Breathing in his familiar, citrus-y scent. But then, a tad reluctantly, they realised they should probably get up – if they wanted to enjoy the "breakfast" part of their bed 'n breakfast stay, that was!

Lacey took a shower in the beautiful bathroom, and felt herself unwind even more thanks to the hot water pounding down on her from the rainfall shower head, and the soothing smell of the complimentary lavender cleansing gel. After that she dressed in jeans, boots and a cosy sweater, and they headed downstairs.

The breakfast room turned out to be yet another gorgeous space in the château. Situated at the back of the building, it was flooded with natural light, thanks to three sets of floor-to-ceiling windows which framed stunning views over the rear moat and the walled garden beyond. Chairs and wooden tables were dotted throughout the space, all dressed with teacups, cutlery and adorable, red *Toile de Jouy* cloth napkins. There was also an enormous, vintage chandelier hanging in the middle of the ceiling; the walls were painted in a chic cranberry shade; and there was a marble fireplace on the far wall that, just like in the salon, had a cheerful holly garland draped across the mantel shelf, in a sweet nod to Christmas.

When Lacey and Daniel walked in, they spotted another two sets of couples already enjoying a morning brew – clearly other guests at the château. They smiled at one another and exchanged greetings. And then Judy arrived, full of smiles, too. After asking if they'd slept well, she popped a pot of hot coffee on their table then set about bringing them breakfast.

For the next little while, Lacey found herself not only enjoying amazing food – a plump fruit salad, made with grapefruit and berries; slice after slice of warm, crusty baguette slathered with butter and local *confiture d'abricot*, apricot jam; a steaming mug of Judy's freshly-pressed coffee. She also found herself feeling like she was floating on air ... probably because she and Daniel couldn't seem to stop grinning soppily at one another across the table! As he mouthed *I love you*, she once again sent out a silent thank you to the universe, that they'd managed to clear the air between them last night. Just in time to *truly* enjoy being together in this romantic setting, so perfect for their anniversary celebrations!

After breakfast, they headed out in the car. Judy had mentioned that there was a popular Christmas market at one of the larger towns, Courlizon, about a half hour drive away; and she and Daniel both immediately decided that sounded like a great way to spend their day!

It was another cold day outside. Their drive took them through peaceful countryside, with wintery views of frost-strewn fields and small pockets of woodland. Eventually they arrived at Courlizon, where they did indeed find a bouncing market taking place in the cobbled town centre!

'Wow, this looks fun,' Daniel remarked, as he pulled on his hat and gloves. Then he took her hand in his, and they made a start on wandering around the bustling stalls. As they did Lacey was reminded of the day she'd spent at the Christmas market with Ella and Lina, back in York. That had been lovely, of course; but it somehow felt even *more* special to get to share the Christmassy experience of a festive market with her husband, given the sadness they'd both felt lately.

The atmosphere was spirited and cheerful. The kiosks were decorated with fairy lights and shiny baubles. At one end of the event they found themselves in a crowd of people, who'd stopped to listen to a local folk group singing lively French songs, accompanied by violins. Which made a very merry backdrop to the market! Then – after applauding with everybody else – they moved on, eyes wide as they took in stand after stand of gifts and decorations, foodstuffs and wine, manned by stallholders wearing thick cardigans and mittens.

It didn't take long before looking turned to shopping. More Christmas shopping, that was! Lacey found a pair of dainty silver earrings for Ella at a jewellery stand, and an ivory silk scarf for Charlotte at another. Daniel snapped up a set of local-made chutneys for Neville; and a *Cointreau* gift pack for Rob. They passed a booth selling *marron grillés* – roasted chestnuts – and inhaled the gorgeously-warming scent; then giggled at the eager throng of shoppers lining up to buy a cup of *vin chaud traditionnel*, or spiced hot wine (Lacey thought that looked the most popular stand of the whole market!).

Eventually, the cold drove them inside, to a café on a nearby street. There, after Daniel reminded her she had to build her strength up, they lunched on delicious pizza and *frites* – balanced out with a healthy side salad, of course!

After their bellies were full, they spent some more time exploring the centre of Courlizon, hand in hand the whole time. They meandered through a local park, and admired the town's old characterful stone buildings and its gothic church. Then, as the sun started to dip and the Christmas lights strung through the streets began to twinkle into the late-afternoon gloom, Lacey found herself enjoying one more treat, back at the market…

It was a treat she hadn't thought she'd get to enjoy this winter: a huge hot chocolate topped with whipped cream and sprinkles! Daniel got one too; and they sat at an outdoor table and both exclaimed how sweet it tasted, given they weren't much used to sugary foods after their mad health drive of late!

On the drive back to the château, Lacey found herself reflecting on what a gorgeously romantic day it had been. Daniel had been so attentive and loving all day long, and it was honestly a relief to see he still felt happy in their marriage, despite the fact no kids had come along yet. It was a relief to see him *looking* happier, too, to see – after their talk last night – that his old, more cheerful, easy-going self still existed. It had just understandably gotten a little lost, a little weighed down by the stress of the past few months.

Of course, Lacey nodded, looking out into the darkness of the countryside as they wove their way back along the lanes to the guesthouse, she knew there were going to be tough times ahead. Once they finally got their appointment with a fertility specialist, who knew what route the consultant would recommend they take, when it came to their baby plans? IVF was looking more and more likely; and she knew, from all the stories she'd read online, that that would be an emotional, uncertain and challenging experience.

They were going to have to hold on to days like today, to bolster them, she realised. To keep them strong. To keep them close … so that they could face *together* whatever the future might bring.

If Lacey thought leaving Courlizon marked the end of her romantic day with her husband, though, she soon realised she was mistaken. Because, as they drove up the bumpy drive towards the château, something happened…

It started snowing!

'Oh, look!' She pointed through the windscreen, at the swirling, twirling snowflakes that suddenly began dancing down from the sky.

Daniel brought the car to a stop. For a moment they just watched, mesmerised, as the pretty white flakes drifted down and began forming an ivory blanket over the grounds of the château. And then he turned to her and grinned.

'Come on. Let's go for a walk.'

A walk? Lacey hesitated, then smiled back. Why not?!

The moment they got out of the car, it felt like a hush had fallen over the world. Daniel tugged her in the direction of the pretty gardens to the side of the building. The gravel pathway crunched underfoot as they walked through the flurry, feeling a child-like delight at the Christmassy twist the weather had taken. Giggling and giddy, they took a turn around the lawn, thrilled to find themselves in the midst of the pirouetting snowflakes.

And then Lacey spotted something else, high above them...

'Daniel, how sweet is that?!'

Visible from this side of the building, there was a Christmas tree, framed in the narrow window of one of the château's many turrets. Its pearly lights twinkled and glistened into the darkness. And set against the falling snow, up there in one of the most romantic parts of the castle, it made such an enchanting sight that Lacey found herself sighing with contentment.

Oh, what a magical place *Le Château de Noël* was! She was certain she'd remember the utter beauty of this moment forever.

They stared at the tree for a moment or two longer, entranced. And then Daniel turned and pulled her into his arms.

They stood there in the crisp, wintery night. Silent. Bodies pressed close. Eyes locked so intensely on one another, that Lacey felt a little breathless.

She loved this man so much. And tingles ran through her, as she thought of how the perfect end, to this perfect day of rekindling their love, would be to feel his lips on hers...

'I love you, Lacey,' he finally uttered. 'I mean, I *really* love you. Whatever happens for us, the fact I've got you as my wife means I'm already the luckiest bloke on the planet. I ... I think I needed this weekend to remind me of that.'

And then, with the snow continuing to tumble around them, he *did* kiss her. It was a kiss that reminded Lacey of when they'd first fallen in love, all those years ago. A hungry, passionate, desperate kiss. A kiss that made her ache inside. A kiss that made her forget the world completely.

It wasn't long before Daniel was gently tugging her back towards the château's front entrance...

'Let's go upstairs.' His voice had turned husky with longing. He took her hand, and she began to follow him. Because suddenly there was nothing in the world she wanted more, than to clamber under the sheets of the pretty antique bedstead in their room, and spend the rest of the night entangled with her gorgeous husband.

Before they did that, though, she realised she wanted to tell him something. Something she thought might make his night even more special...

'Daniel? It's the right time. For ... for trying, I mean,' she murmured. Her fertility app had told her that, right before they'd come on this trip.

He stopped in his tracks. But when he turned back to look at her, she noticed he was shaking his head.

'Oh, Lace. I don't care about that! I mean, *I do*. Of course I do. But not tonight.' He shot her a slow, sexy smile, before pulling her close again and nuzzling her neck, in a way that sent her pulse racing.

'Tonight,' he murmured, 'I just want you. Nothing else. I just want to be with my wife. I want to show you what you mean to me.'

Lacey melted into his arms. And as they made their way into the guesthouse, and climbed the staircase to their room, she couldn't help the soppy smile that filled her face.

Given how much she knew her husband wanted a baby – and all the worries she'd been harbouring about whether he could still be happy in a marriage without kids – what he'd just said to her meant the world. It really did. In fact, it made the words he'd just uttered, about simply wanting to be with her tonight, some of the most romantic he'd ever sent her way!

As he laid her down on the bed and covered her with kisses, her heart flooded with gladness and love.

SIXTEEN

Later, much later, Daniel woke with a start in their château bedroom. He glanced around, almost certain he'd been disturbed by a strange noise – from *inside* the room.

By the far wall, a lamp on the dresser was giving out a small pool of light. Enough for him to see that the room was still. Quiet. There was nothing obvious that could be responsible for disturbing the contented sleep he'd fallen into, after he'd brought Lacey to bed and shown her just how much he still wanted her. How much he still adored her.

On that note, he turned to look at his wife. She was still napping, hair all around her on the pillow. There was a peaceful look on her face, that made him smile, dreamily, and want to reach out and gently stroke her cheek.

Before he could do that, though ... there it was again. That noise.

Now he was fully awake, he realised what it was.

It was a giggle. A girlish, playful giggle, the likes of which he'd heard only a few days earlier, back at Grace Hall.

Cécile?

His head whipped back towards the foot of the bed. Sure enough, this time he caught sight of a shimmering light. It fluttered around, as though trying to catch his attention. And then it darted towards the door, disappearing into the hallway beyond.

Daniel blinked in surprise. But then, realising the light clearly wanted him to follow it, he scrambled quietly out of bed and pulled on his discarded jeans and jumper. After all, if it *was* Cécile dancing around the property, he was eager to take this chance to thank her. Because look at the gift she'd given him – and Lacey, too! He'd never have known about this amazing château without her intervention. Would never have thought to bring his wife to such a pretty place, and use the mini-break as a way of apologising to her for his pushy and aloof behaviour of late.

Maybe, he thought wryly, as he tiptoed to the door, it paid to have friends in the spirit world. Because in these past weeks not only had wise Wilfred stepped in to show him his relationship was heading down a dark path; but little Cécile had played a huge part in helping him return his marriage to a place of love and togetherness. It was a thought that made him feel very blessed indeed!

Out in the corridor, the light was hovering, waiting for him. As soon as he emerged from the bedroom, it headed down the hall. He glanced around – the landing was quiet, thankfully, allowing him to dart along the cream carpet in pursuit.

They turned a corner, passed a cute window seat, a slender sideboard topped with a matching pair of brass lamps ... and then the light disappeared through a half-open door.

It was only then that Daniel hesitated. He stared at the doorway in front of him. Should he really go poking around the Millers' home like this? He *could* see – because the door was ajar enough for him to peer through the opening – that it certainly didn't lead on to a personal space, like a bedroom. So he wouldn't be disturbing the other guests or anything like that.

And then he remembered: Judy had said they should feel free to explore the château, hadn't she? *We leave the doors open to rooms you can take a peek at*, he suddenly recalled her saying, on their arrival.

That settled it then. He quickly stepped forward ... and found himself on another landing. This landing was only small, though. And it led to only one place – a narrow spiral staircase at the far end.

Assuming the light had to have shimmied up those very stairs, Daniel started heading towards them. He'd only taken a step or two, though, when he came to a stop once more. Because, suddenly, there she was! Standing by the foot of the staircase, in her frilly white dress: Cécile! She looked really quite hazy, not fully formed at all. But he could see enough of her to know she was smiling, and that there was a look of joy all over her adorable little face.

'Monsieur Daniel! *Bonsoir.* And – look! I found a way to visit you, here at my old home! I will be very tired when I return to my mama, but it will be worth it.' She looked round, to where there was a small window behind her, and peered out at the moat and snow-covered gardens below, before sighing longingly.

'Now you are here, you must understand, *non*?' she murmured quietly. 'Why I loved this château so dearly?' She turned back to him and pressed a little hand to her chest. '*En effet*, it is more beautiful, I believe, than you could even have imagined?'

'Oh, Cécile. It's an amazing place,' he told her earnestly. Then, worried her half-translucent state meant she might disappear at any moment, he went on to thank her. To thank her for the way she'd come back into his life to help him. For the gift she'd given him, of showing him this special place existed, and of knowing a trip here would be the perfect way of bringing him and Lacey close again.

'I can't thank you enough. You are one very kind little girl, that's for sure.'

She clapped her hands in delight at that compliment. 'Oh, *merci*, Daniel!' She smiled, then tilted her head and stared at him, serious once more.

'*Alors,* you are happy again? I was correct to think my home would bring you what you need?'

'Yes. It most definitely has,' he nodded.

'*Bon.* This makes *me* very happy to hear. *Maintenant.* Listen carefully, Daniel.' She pointed towards the top of the spiral staircase, then shot him a knowing smile. 'Do you hear? Someone is calling you. You should not leave them waiting any longer...'

Daniel frowned. Um, really? He listened carefully ... but his ears were only met with silence. Was his little friend mistaken? Who on earth would be calling his name from the top of the stairs, anyway? Judy or Larry, perhaps, wondering what he was doing loitering down here?

He didn't get a chance to ask Cécile any of those questions, though ... because, in front of his very eyes, her hazy figure began to shrink back into the form of a radiant light.

'It was so lovely to see you again. But now I must say: *au revoir,* dearest Daniel.'

Softly, slowly, she disappeared, leaving the landing still and empty. And leaving Daniel confused, into the bargain.

They'd only spent mere moments together, this time around. But it had been long enough for him to thank Cécile for bringing him to her charming home, and he was grateful for that.

He couldn't pretend he didn't feel a little rattled by her parting words, though...

Someone is calling you. You should not leave them waiting any longer.

For a moment Daniel just stood there, nervously wringing his hands. And then, slowly, he edged towards the staircase. He peered up the twisting steps, but could see only darkness spiralling above him.

He swallowed, then drew back his shoulders. Cécile had clearly wanted him to climb these steps. So he was going to have to trust her and do just that, wasn't he?

Carefully, with a firm grip of the thick rope handrail, he took the stairs one at a time. Eventually, he reached another doorway.

Once again, the door before him was ajar. Unlike the gloomy staircase, he noticed there was a light on inside the room, because its brightness was spilling out through the gap. Did that mean there *was* somebody inside, already?

He cleared his throat. Called out a tentative *Hello?*

Nobody answered. So, carefully, he pushed the door fully open. It slid back with a creak ... and Daniel instantly realised where he was.

It was the circular shape of the room, plus the glistening Christmas tree in one of the two narrow windows that gave it away: this was the gorgeous turret room he and Lacey had been staring up at from the gardens earlier, wasn't it?!

He walked through the doorway, intrigued to take a closer look at the unusual room. He was just about to admire its cosy armchairs; the slim walnut bookcase stuffed with vintage volumes set against one wall; the handsome Moroccan lamp hanging from the ceiling ... when he abruptly realised he actually couldn't care less about any of those – admittedly chic – details.

How *could* he focus on the room's décor – when he'd suddenly noticed there *was* another person in the small space with him?!

That other person was a man. A man, who was standing by the second window. Daniel's first thought was that it was Larry, and that he was disturbing the owner of the château by snooping around up here.

But then he noticed *this* particular bloke was tall and, unlike their lovely host, was clean-shaven and had a thick head of dark hair. He was also dressed in clothes that looked a little old-fashioned: dark trousers, paired with a nineties-esque, loose-fitting shirt and a twill coat.

Finally, there was a strangely fond expression on the man's face, that seemed to grow with intensity as he looked directly across the room at Daniel...

Daniel froze. His heart began beating hard in his chest as he realised he *knew* this face that was staring right at him...

He knew it well. *So* well.

It was a face he saw often, you see – in the photographs dotted all over his mum's house. It was a face that'd lived on in his memory, for many years now.

'Dad?!'

No. It couldn't be. In fact, Daniel could hardly believe he was uttering that word. He rubbed at his eyes with trembling hands. Gave himself a little shake.

But he *wasn't* mistaken. It really was his father, Henry, who was hovering there by the window.

Time seemed to stop. Outside the windows, snow continued to fall. And, inside, Daniel and his dad continued to stare across the small space at one another.

Henry didn't say a word. But his fond look turned to a smile. Daniel realised it seemed like his dad was in the room; yet not in the room, all at the same time. As though he was standing behind some kind of gauzy screen. And the smile that appeared on his face – it was soft, but full of affection.

Tears pricked at his eyes. His heart fluttered and panged. He felt almost like he was a little boy again, and wanted to run to his dad, throw his arms around him, and tell him how much he'd missed him all these years.

But he didn't do that. For fear of disturbing the moment, he didn't do *anything*. Because it wasn't even supposed to be possible, for his dad to be here like this, was it? Not when *he* hadn't spent time in the hazy realm between earth and the afterlife, like Wilfred and Cécile had. Perhaps, Daniel wondered, his spirit friends had played a hand in bringing Henry here tonight?

Either way, he just stood there – for what felt like hours, but in reality was probably only seconds – and soaked in the loving, fatherly presence that'd been absent from his life for so long.

And then Henry lifted a hand and pointed, towards one of the armchairs in the room. Clearly, he wanted to show Daniel something.

But Daniel hesitated before moving his eyes in the direction his dad was indicating. The reason being, out of the blue a strange sound hit his ears.

It was a *nice* sound. Like a ... a happy babbling noise, he realised.

Exactly the kind of noise, in fact, that a contented baby would make...

He snapped his head around. What he saw on the armchair by the far wall made his eyes grow wide.

Lacey. *Lacey* was sitting in the chair.

But ... how was that possible?!

Not only that – there was something in her arms.

His jaw dropped as he clocked what it was.

A baby. His wife had a teeny-tiny baby, with a sprinkling of black hair, and little pink cheeks, nestled close to her chest. It was gurgling delightedly up at her. And she was cooing and smiling back at it, with a look of such bliss on her face, Daniel's heart nearly burst.

What was going on? Whose baby *was that*? he nearly yelped aloud.

When he looked back in confusion at his dad, he saw that Henry's smile had changed. It had turned from one of softness ... to one of delight. As though ... well, as though he was full of gladness, at getting to give his son a gift he knew he'd love.

In that moment, Daniel was filled with the strangest sensation. He held his dad's gaze for a beat longer. And then, as he turned back to the vision of his wife holding that tiny precious bundle, a feeling of peace washed over him.

A feeling of letting go. A feeling of contentment, the likes of which he hadn't felt in a long, long time.

Suddenly, he just knew.

It had been a difficult year.

But everything was going to be OK.

*

'Daniel? Are you in there? Oh–'

Lacey peeked tentatively around the door at the top of the spiral staircase she'd just climbed. Sure enough, she found her husband in the small room beyond. Relieved, she stumbled through the doorway, keen to check he was OK.

She'd spotted him, mere minutes earlier, you see, leaving their bedroom. She'd woken, to see him heading out the door and, wondering where he was going, had called out to him. But he'd seemed strangely distracted – *too* distracted – to hear her. And there'd been a strange, almost trance-like look on his face, that'd sparked a beat of concern in her. To the point she'd slid out of bed and, after locating her discarded clothes, followed after him.

He'd got a head start on her, but when she'd reached the door at the end of the cream-carpeted corridor – the one that led to the spiral staircase – it was clear there was no other place he could have gone, than up those winding steps.

And now here they were.

'Daniel, are you OK? What are you doing up here–'

She broke off, distracted, suddenly. The reason being, as she stepped inside, she realised she recognised the room they were in.

This was the very same turret room they'd seen from the gardens below, wasn't it?! It had to be, given the dazzling Christmas tree set by the window.

That wasn't the only thing that caught her attention, though...

She looked around, and felt really quite mesmerised by the romantic vibe of the small space she found herself in. To start with, the fact it was a *turret* room gave it a unique charm, of course. And the décor – a couple of comfy-looking armchairs, a Moroccan lantern, the thick woven rug set atop the parquet floor. That was all gorgeous, too. It made the room seem like the sort of place you could retreat to, with a good book and a hot mug of tea, to escape the world for a while.

But the main thing that struck Lacey about the space ... was the almost magical atmosphere hanging in the air. Walking into it felt like walking into a warm hug. In fact, it felt more like a chamber than a room. A snug, cosy chamber that enveloped you and made you feel safe and at ease.

'Oh, Daniel. I didn't think this château could get any more perfect. But this has to be my favourite room of all!'

She expected her husband to grin and agree – he loved interior design, after all, so this space had to have made quite the impression on him, too.

But he didn't say anything. In fact, as she smiled at him, she realised Daniel might be standing right in front of her ... but he didn't even seem to notice she was there. He was too busy staring across the room, with a soppy smile on his face. Actually, he was more than staring. He looked ... *transfixed*.

Lacey frowned. She recalled the odd look that'd been on his face when he'd left their bedroom, too. Then she glanced round again, trying to see what had caught his attention so completely. But all she could see what was she'd just described: a chic, lovely room with a few pieces of stylish furniture and an enchanting vibe.

'*Daniel?*' she tried again, at the same time tugging gently on his sleeve.

This time, he started. Finally, he looked at her, and it was like a mist clearing behind his eyes.

He still didn't say anything, though. Instead, he swiftly returned his gaze to the other side of the room. As he did, he blinked, and suddenly didn't look spellbound any longer. Instead, something almost bittersweet seemed to cross his face.

'Um.' She scratched her head. 'Sweetheart, is everything alright?'

It took another moment or two before he slowly nodded his head. And then, with a little sigh, he returned his gaze to her.

'Lacey.' He pulled her tightly to his chest.

'Lacey,' he said again, whispering into her hair. 'I have to tell you something.'

He did? She drew her head back and looked up at him, noticing his eyes were strangely bright.

'You might think this is a bit weird but ... I've just had this feeling. That, one way or another, everything's going to work out for us.'

And Lacey wasn't sure if it was the warmth of her husband's arms, or the love shining in his eyes. Or whether it was being in this romantic turret room, or the prettiness of the twinkling tree next to them. Or if it was the shimmering snowflakes still tumbling down outside.

But she suddenly felt it too. It might sound strange, but there was something in the air, wasn't there? A sweet sense, that the long, hard year they'd had, was eventually going to lead to something amazing...

With her heart soothed and filled with hope, she snuggled back against her husband's chest ... and just knew it was going to be a wonderful Christmas, after all!

***

Author Note

Thank you for reading **Lacey and the Christmas Château**.

I very much hope you enjoyed the book. If you did, could you possibly leave a review on Amazon or Goodreads?

Your thoughts and feedback are much valued, and help others decide if they might enjoy the **Lacey's World** series.

Thank you for your time, wonderful readers! ☺

More Lacey and Daniel adventures will be on the way soon...

In the meantime, if you'd like to read another of my works, you can meet Hannah and Harry in **The Summer of Broken Hearts**, available on Amazon now!

And please do follow me on Instagram for updates on future releases!

@jenniferpotterauthor

Much love,

Jennifer x

ALSO BY JENNIFER POTTER

Lacey's Dilemma

Lacey's Secret

The Summer of Broken Hearts

Printed in Dunstable, United Kingdom